"What v
set on y

His meaning was unmistakable, and Cassy's eyes flashed blue flame. "I *beg* your pardon?" she demanded in a voice that would strip paint.

"Or are you holding out for the highest bid?" James persisted provocatively. "A wedding ring perhaps?"

"What's wrong with that?" she returned with disdain.

He shook his head. "What a pity," he murmured. "I'm not prepared to bid that high. But that doesn't mean I'm not interested in what's on offer. I don't suppose you'd be prepared to negotiate?"

Cassy had to fight to suppress the tide of anger that was seething inside her. "You—you want me to be your *mistress*?" she demanded, stunned.

That fatally attractive smile curved his hard mouth. "Mistress—what a delightfully old-fashioned name for it," he taunted softly, his dark eyes caressing her, making her skin flame. "But I like it. So—yes, I want you to be my mistress."

SUSANNE McCARTHY has spent most of her life in Lond
but after her marriage she and her husband moved to
Shropshire. The author is now an enthusiastic advocate
this unspoiled part of England, and although she has se
her novels in other locations, Susanne says that the
English countryside may feature in her future writing.

Books by Susanne McCarthy

Don't miss any of our special offers. Write to us at the
following address for information on our newest releases.

Harlequin Reader Service
901 Fuhrmann Blvd., P.O. Box 1397, Buffalo, NY 14240
Canadian address: P.O. Box 603,
Fort Erie, Ont. L2A 5X3

SUSANNE McCARTHY

caught in a dream

Harlequin Books

TORONTO • NEW YORK • LONDON
AMSTERDAM • PARIS • SYDNEY • HAMBURG
STOCKHOLM • ATHENS • TOKYO • MILAN

Harlequin Presents first edition February 1989
ISBN 0-373-11146-0

Original hardcover edition published in 1988
by Mills & Boon Limited

CHAPTER ONE

'LOT number one hundred and thirty-three, ladies and gentlemen. May I call your attention to this very elegant English rosewood *bonheur-de-jour* in the Sheraton style, made in 1780. A lovely piece, I think you will agree. Bidding in increments of one hundred, please. May I begin at five thousand? You, sir—thank you.'

The auctioneer accepted a purely imaginary bid, a little below the reserve price, and watched with satisfaction as the early bids ran the price up, confident that the desk would easily reach the estimate set on it earlier.

At just under ten thousand dollars the buyer from Rhoda Hutton's came in, lifting her catalogue a fraction of an inch in the precise but discreet signal of the experienced customer. The auctioneer smiled to himself as he took her bid—he had expected her to be interested in this piece. She had the instincts of a true expert, though she was remarkably young; twenty-five, maybe—with that sort of poise it wasn't easy to tell.

She was English, of course, and her grandfather was a lord, so she would have grown up with the finest things around her. It was easy to recognise the pedigree—she had that willowy English-rose beauty that could never be counterfeited. Her skin was as translucent as porcelain, her features as delicately moulded, and she wore her silver-blonde hair in a sleek coil at the nape of her neck.

There was a smile of satisfaction in those fine sapphire-blue eyes. The price was hovering at eleven thousand dollars—all the absentee-bids in the book had been left behind, and those in the sale-room were drying up. She was going to get the desk—and at a good price, too.

But suddenly someone else caught the auctioneer's eye. Sir James Clayton was so subtle in his bids that no one else in the sale-room guessed that it was he that was calling. Not that anyone could have read his intentions—he had the face of a poker-player, giving nothing away.

The auctioneer found himself siding with the lady, hoping she would win. Sir James was a highly valued customer, of course, on the rare occasions when he came into the sale-room himself, but he had the reputation of being a predator, both in business and in pursuing his hobby of collecting antiques. You could see that in his face—a certain shrewdness in those dark eyes, a suggestion of ruthlessness in the line of his jaw.

'I have eleven thousand five hundred dollars. To you, Miss Durward?'

Sir James glanced round, startled, as he heard her name. Cassy smiled to herself. She had guessed that he hadn't recognised her before. It was hardly surprising, of course—she hadn't seen him for years. Though they were distantly related, and virtually next-door neighbours in the sleepy Somerset village that was home, she had lived in New York for six years now, and didn't get home as much as she would like. And there had been no love lost between the Durwards and the Claytons for many years.

It was her bid. Something in those dark eyes told her that it was he who had been bidding against her. She hesitated for a fraction of a second. Eleven and a half thousand was the limit she had agreed with Rhoda. Oh, if only she could go on bidding—purely for the satisfaction of beating James Clayton. She would even put her own money towards it . . . But that would just be foolish, so regretfully she shook her head.

The auctioneer flashed her a sympathetic smile, and raised his gavel. 'Eleven thousand five hundred dollars I have. Are there any more bids?' His eyes swept the room in vain. 'For the first time . . . For the second time . . .' The gavel came down with a sharp clack, and the tension in the air eased with a flurry of coughing and scraping of chairs. 'Sold to Sir James Clayton. Lot number one hundred and thirty-four . . .'

Cassy rose to her feet, and rolling up her catalogue edged out of the row of chairs. It was a pity about the writing-desk, but still . . .

'I'm sorry if you're disappointed.'

She handed in her paddle to the porter in the doorway, and turned to look up at her erstwhile rival. 'Not at all,' she responded coolly. 'I think perhaps eleven and a half thousand was a little too high—though it's a nice enough desk, I suppose.'

His dark eyes flickered with amusement at the faint hint of mockery in her voice. 'Nice enough for you to have bid all the way,' he pointed out with maddening insouciance. She permitted herself a minimal smile. 'You know, I didn't recognise you to begin with,' he went on. 'But then I should imagine the last time I saw you, you were still a skinny schoolgirl. You've done a bit of growing up since then.'

His eyes slid down over her slender figure in undisguised appreciation. She tilted her chin at a proud angle, confident that he would never guess that the well cut suit of French navy linen had been bought from one of those useful little shops where the very rich sold their nearly-new cast-offs, as had the scarlet silk blouse she wore beneath it.

'It would certainly be several years since we last met,' she concurred.

He fell into step with her as she walked briskly down the stairs. 'What are you doing for lunch?' he enquired.

'I'm sorry, I rarely stop for lunch.'

'But you must stop for breath,' he countered irrepressibly. 'Or at least for coffee. Come on, you've lived in New York too long. Five minutes out of your schedule won't bring the world to an end—you'd have had to hang around longer than that if you'd bought the desk.' He took her arm, and steered her towards the coffee-lounge on the first floor.

He hadn't changed a bit, Cassy thought wryly. She could remember vividly the way the girls in the village used to sigh over those dark good looks, and tell in whispers and giggles of the dangers of letting him coax you into going for a ride in his powerful sports car.

'So,' he said as they found themselves an empty table in the smart coffee-bar, 'what are you doing in New York?'

'I work for a dealer,' she told him. 'Just round the corner from here—Rhoda Hutton.'

'Oh yes, I know her. How is she these days? Still paying way over the odds for Tiffany glass?'

Cassy laughed. 'Yes, I'm afraid she is—it's her big weakness.'

'Is that who you were buying the desk for?'

'Yes. She's going to be disappointed to have lost it.' She slanted him a speculative smile. 'I don't suppose you'd be willing to . . . negotiate?'

He lifted an enquiring eyebrow. 'What are you prepared to offer?'

'What would you be asking?' she returned cagily.

'I'm not sure that I want to sell it.'

She searched his eyes, not sure if he was fencing with her. 'You'd be making an instant profit,' she pointed out.

'What makes you think I'd be interested in that?'

Because you're a Clayton, she thought. But though she didn't say it aloud, she couldn't keep the irony from her voice as she enquired, 'Aren't you?'

'Not particularly.'

'Oh, come on, Sir James,' she prompted, simulating a worldly cynicism. 'Everything has its price.' He really was an infuriating man, sitting there with that mocking glint in his eyes. He was making her play devil's advocate—she deeply envied the private collector, who could disregard the profit motive and buy for pure love of beauty and craftsmanship.

'Does it, indeed?' he returned, lifting one sardonic eyebrow. 'Then I'll tell you my price for considering your offer—have dinner with me tonight.'

She blinked at him in astonishment. 'I beg your pardon?'

He lifted his eyebrows in mock surprise. 'I thought they still spoke a kind of English in New York,' he teased. 'Dinner—you know, the last meal of the day.'

'There's no need for a translation,' she retorted coldly. Of all the nerve . . .! 'I'm sorry, Sir James, but I'm afraid I couldn't possibly.' She cast a swift glance at her watch. 'I'm afraid I really am in rather a hurry. If you'll excuse me.'

She rose to her feet. He made no attempt to detain her further. She hurried down the stairs and squeezed her way through the gossiping knot of dealers gathered around the main entrance. He really did have a cheek, she thought angrily, as she stepped out into the bustle of Park Avenue. As if she'd agree to have dinner with him, just to persuade him to part with that desk!

'I'm sorry, Rhoda, I didn't get it.'

Rhoda looked disappointed. 'What did it go for?' Cassy told her. 'Ah, well—it couldn't really be called a bargain at that price. Who bought it?'

'Sir James Clayton.'

Rhoda's thick false eyelashes batted in astonishment. '*The* James Clayton? Oh, I wish I'd gone myself now! He's just *gorgeous!*'

Cassy gurgled with laughter. 'Rhoda, you are one very susceptible lady. You fall for them all!'

'No, I don't,' her employer protested indignantly. 'But he *is* a most charming man. I met him last year in Miami. So good-looking, and all that money . . .!'

'Did you know his family fortune was based on stewed apples?' queried Cassy drily.

Rhoda looked suitably intrigued. 'Really? How did you know that?'

'He comes from Somerset too.'

'Oh? So you know him quite well, then?'

'Fairly well,' conceded Cassy evasively.

Rhoda slanted her a look of speculative enquiry. 'Uh-huh? And will you be seeing him when you go home?'

'I doubt it. I dare say he's quite a busy man, and I'm probably going to be pretty tied up myself. Heaven only knows what Grandpa's up to—I could barely read a word of that letter.'

'Well, I hope it's nothing real bad, honey. You will be back in time for my little shindig next month, won't you? Now, promise, Cassy. I know you and Craig . . .'

Cassy shook her head, laughing. 'There's no ill-feeling, Rhoda—certainly not on my side. Craig and I are still very good friends—but we wouldn't have stayed that way if we had got married, now would we? And besides,' she added teasingly, 'it would have meant having you for a mother-in-law!'

It took Rhoda a second or two to realise that she was joking, and then she chuckled with laughter. 'Well, I won't say it isn't a disappointment,' she commented with a sigh. 'I *did* hope he'd find himself a nice girl this time—third time lucky, you know.'

'Rhoda, there are a million girls in New York who'd give their right arm for a man like your son, so don't worry—he won't stay on the shelf for

long. Now, I must dash—I've got a heap of things
to do if I'm going to catch that plane.'

Rather less than twenty-four hours after she had
bumped into Sir James Clayton in the auction-
rooms, Cassy was landing at Heathrow. It was
odd, she reflected, that she should meet someone
from home like that, just the day before she was
coming over.

From London she caught the train. Fortunately
it wasn't too crowded, and she managed to get a
corner seat. She couldn't suppress a secret smile of
self-mockery at her reflection in the window—
when she was a little girl, it had always been an
omen of good luck if she had managed to get the
corner seat on the train home, a guarantee of a
good holiday.

It hadn't been the Inter-City from London then,
of course, just the local from her boarding-school
near Gloucester. And holidays had always been
good. Grandpa's house had had a sort of fairy-tale
quality to her as a child—it had been the only real
home she had known.

Her parents had died ten years ago, in a flying
accident in France, but she hadn't really missed
them. They had always travelled a lot; for the first
eight years of her life she had trailed around the
world with them, from Val D'Iser to Mustique,
cared for by a series of au pairs. But she had
needed to go to school, so eventually she had been
sent home to England.

She hadn't been happy at school—the newspapers had often been full of nasty stories about
her parents and their friends, and the other girls
could sometimes be very cruel. But she had only

had to close her eyes and wish, and she could be transported to her Somerset home, and all her troubles would be solved as if by magic.

A fairy-tale world, peopled by fairy-tale characters. Grandpa, old and wise, full of stories, always hiding a secret treat for his 'little blue-eyed girl'. Fishy, the plump old housekeeper, in her kitchen full of golden pastries and dark plum cakes. Even Jenkins, who was valet and chauffeur as well as butler, always as stately and proper as if he were still presiding over the 'Big House', but always with a pocketful of toffee for little Miss Cassy. All living together in a tall old house on the edge of the village, in a state of genteel poverty.

Once upon a time, Grandpa had been rich. He had owned land and property throughout the valley, and lived in the beautiful old manor-house that overlooked the village. But he had been swindled out of his fortune many years ago by his own brother-in-law, Sir Giles Clayton—James's grandfather.

Sir Giles, too, had been a fairy-tale character of her childhood—the Wicked Baron. He hadn't quite been a real baron—just a baronet, elevated to the lower echelons of the peerage in the nineteen-fifties for his services to industry or something. He had died about five years ago—in spite of all Grandpa's imprecations he had died peacefully in his bed, at the ripe old age of eighty-six, surrounded by his loving family.

His grandson had inherited the vast fortune he had built. Tere Valley Produce was a big inter-national company now—it was funny to think that it had been started on two hundred acres leased from her great-grandfather. And he had inherited

the title too, of course. Cassy smiled to herself.
James Clayton was perfectly cast in the role of
Wicked Baron . . .

Impatiently she shook thoughts of James
Clayton from her head, and reached into her bag
for the letter that had brought her home. It was
impossible to read Grandpa's scrawl. Was that
'ultimate'? It could be 'desperate' if that was a 'p'.
Dear Grandpa. What on earth was going on? It
was worrying, being so far away from him—he had
been a vigorous seventy-three when she had left,
but each time she visited she was aware that he was
growing older. Maybe it was time she thought
about coming back to England for good.

She hadn't set out to go to America, or even to
make a career in antiques. She had simply been
helping out a friend in an antiques shop in Bath,
the summer after she had left school. And then
Rhoda had swept into her life like a tornado, and
made her an offer she couldn't refuse. She hadn't
cared that Cassy had no formal training in
antiques—she had a feel for them that couldn't be
taught, she had declared.

And so Cassy had gone to New York, to work in
the chic showroom in the heart of Manhattan. It
had been hard work, but she had loved it, and
Rhoda had taught her everything she knew. Now
she had virtually taken over the buying side, and
she rarely had a moment to herself.

She was very fond of Rhoda, but she had only
been half joking when she had said she didn't want
her for a mother-in-law. Her son was a lovely man;
he was a wine-shipper, very cultured and good-
looking, charming and gentle—but sometimes
Cassy felt that he was actually *looking* for a wife

as bossy as his mother. His first two wives had given up in despair, unable to cope with Rhoda.

Cassy had been going out with him for about three years, on and off, and they had been drifting towards marriage. But she had increasingly found herself organising him the way Rhoda did—and she had a horrible feeling that in the end she would grow to be just like her.

The journey from London took just over an hour. The train pulled into the grand neo-classical station at Bath Spa, and disgorged its load of passengers. Several heads turned to watch the coolly elegant blonde as she stepped down from the carriage. She glanced around for a porter, but there were none, so with a rueful sigh she turned to lift her heavy suitcase down from the train.

'Allow me.'

She glanced up in surprise. Sir James Clayton had just stepped down from one of the first-class compartments, and he slanted her a sardonic smile as he picked up her case without waiting for her reply. 'You didn't tell me you were coming home,' he remarked, an inflection of sardonic humour in his voice. 'I didn't see you on the plane.'

'I didn't fly Concorde,' she returned drily.

He smiled—he really did have a very attractive smile. 'How long are you staying?' he asked her.

'Three weeks.'

'Then perhaps we could manage that dinner-date some time?'

'I'm sorry,' she responded without hesitation. 'I've come down to visit my grandfather, not to socialise.'

They had reached the end of the platform, and Cassy had spotted a tall, distinguished-looking old gentleman waiting on the far side of the gate. She raised her hand to wave to him, and eased her way quickly through the knot of people at the ticket-barrier. 'Grandpa!' she cried happily, hurrying up to him. 'You shouldn't have come all this way just to meet me!'

'What, not meet my only granddaughter, when she's coming home after all this time? Don't be silly—I haven't got one foot in the grave yet!' he declared in noble tones. 'Besides, I was up this way anyway.'

Cassy laughed, leaning forward to kiss his paper-thin cheek. 'I should have guessed! How are you? You're looking very well—I didn't know what to expect after reading that letter.'

'Oh, I'm fine—never felt better . . . not that I'm getting any younger, mind you,' he added as an afterthought. 'But let me look at you.' He held her at arm's length. 'Oh, you're even prettier than ever— more like my dearest Elizabeth with every year that passes.' He put up his hand to the corner of his eye to brush away a purely imaginary tear—a dear, familiar gesture. But suddenly his smile turned to a scowl as James approached.

'You have a car waiting?' he enquired, impeccably polite.

'Of course we do, young man,' Grandpa informed him frostily.

'Then allow me to carry your granddaughter's suitcase out to it,' he responded, unperturbed. 'It's rather heavy for her to manage.'

Grandpa's face was growing ominously red. 'Ill-bred young puppy,' he muttered crossly to Cassy. 'What were you thinking of, letting him make up to you?'

'I wasn't, Grandpa,' she explained patiently. 'I didn't see him until I got off the train, and he just offered to carry my bag for me, that's all. And I was very grateful,' she added, a chiding note in her voice. 'It *is* heavy.'

'Why didn't you get a porter?' he demanded.

'I couldn't find one.'

She took his arm firmly, and led him out of the station. It was a beautiful afternoon, almost May, and the pavement outside the station was drifted with white blossom from the trees in the riverside gardens further up the road. Cassy breathed in with a deep sigh of contentment. 'Mmm. Even the *air* smells different.'

Her glance rested with delight on a gleaming old Rolls-Royce parked in the space marked 'Taxis only', and the stiff figure in a peaked cap that stood beside it. 'Jenkins!' she greeted the elderly chauffeur, squeezing his hands. 'You're looking splendid! And so is Adelaide,' she added, running her eyes admiringly over the elegant old car.

'Of course, Miss Cassy,' replied the chauffeur solemnly. 'Adelaide and I just keep going, growing old together.'

'And how is Fishy?'

Jenkins frowned at her use of the deplored nickname. 'Mrs Fisher is very well,' he reproved her, but the sternness of his tone was belied by the twinkle in his eyes.

James had put her case into the boot of the car, and he turned to her, a faintly mocking smile curving his hard mouth. 'Well, good afternoon, then, Miss Durward,' he said, offering her his hand.

Cassy hesitated, oddly reluctant to concede even

the formal physical contact of a handshake. 'Good afternoon,' she said, brushing his fingers briefly with her own.

James nodded politely to Grandpa, and then he turned away, blending with but not quite absorbed by the stream of people leaving the station—his dark head was just a little above those around him, and something about his lithe frame seemed to draw the eye. But Grandpa was waiting to hand her into the car with all his old-fashioned gallantry, and she sank back against the leather seat with a sigh of contentment.

'I'm glad you've still got Adelaide,' she murmured as Jenkins slipped the well preserved engine into gear.

'Of course,' declared Grandpa expansively. 'I couldn't part with her. A gentleman must have a conveyance that suits his position in the world. I don't mind what other economies I have to make to support it.'

'Like not purchasing a tax disc. Or an insurance certificate,' put in Jenkins with all the familiarity of many years of loyal service to his incorrigible employer.

'Oh, don't fuss. You're getting to be a real old woman, with your nagging and your rheumatism. Who is going to arrest *me,* pray?'

Jenkins caught Cassy's eye in the rear-view mirror, and twinkled with dry humour. She smiled in response. Grandpa hadn't changed a bit!

Within a few moments they were on the outskirts of Bath, and heading south-west along the old Roman road. Cassy gazed happily out of the window as the rich, rolling hills of Somerset unfolded around them, sparkling green in the afternoon sunshine, the hedgerows alive with wild flowers.

'Oh, it's so nice to be home!' she sighed contentedly. 'I don't think there's anywhere on earth as beautiful as this.'

Grandpa gave her hand an affectionate squeeze. 'I'm glad to hear you say that. You're a Durward all right. The love of your native soil is in your blood.'

Cassy smiled secretly at the sad irony of his words. Edwin Durward, the Right Honourable the Viscount Bradley, was every inch the aristocrat—comparative poverty had not one whit diminished his air of consequence. His stately figure was still unbowed by almost eighty years, his blue eyes were still sharp. And he still insisted on behaving as if he was Lord of the Manor, driving around in the elegant old Rolls—though he only used it now to impress the villagers on his occasional visits to church, or to go to race-meetings.

His adored wife having died barely a year after their marriage, he had never had time to learn how he would have been bored by the constraints of connubial bliss, and how she would have objected to his ever-present brandy and his pungent cigars. He had reverted very quickly to the habits of his bachelor days, his year governed by the sporting calendar, and consoled himself for his loss by living a life of glorious self-indulgence.

The car purred along, through Midsomer Norton and Shepton Mallet. At last she could see the sparkling River Tere below them, and then the village of Coombe Bradley came into view, clustered around the square tower of the church, the grey stone houses blending perfectly with the setting because the blocks had been carved from these very hills.

And there was the 'Big House'—Bradley Park. Every time she saw it, she was struck by its beauty. In her childhood dreams it had been a fairy-tale palace. It wasn't really a palace, of course, but a graceful Palladian villa of moderate size, built of the same light grey stone as the village. It sat like a queen on the skirt of the hill, surrounded by its wooded parkland.

Though she had never lived there, Cassy knew the grounds very well—as a child she had often slipped out of the gate at the bottom of Grandpa's garden, and up a rough path through the trees to a small wicket-gate, well hidden by ivy, that seemed to have been forgotten. She had crept inside many times, to play solitary games of imagination in which she was a fairy princess, held captive by the Wicked Baron. She had never shown any of her friends where to find the secret gate—it was her special place, and the noisy games of the village children would have spoiled the magic.

Nothing had changed since those childhood days. The sleepy village was exactly as it had always been; the grey stone houses with their neatly kept front gardens, the self-important little shops, the smiling faces of the friends and neighbours who waved to her in greeting.

Over the river, up the hill, and . . . really home. The tall house stood alone at the edge of the village, like a 'distressed gentlewoman', too proud in her poverty to draw closer to her neighbours. The unkempt state of the garden bore witness to the lack of a full-time gardener, and the peeling paint on the window-frames would need attention before many more winters had taken their toll.

The air of sad neglect was heightened by the

entrance-hall. The rich oak panelling was scuffed and faded, the heavy antique sideboard had become a repository for old magazines and unpaid bills. Cassy gazed around in dismay. Poor Fishy really couldn't manage all the housework on her own any more. Grandpa ought to get a girl in from the village—she would speak to him about it later.

Then up from the kitchen regions came the sound of shuffling footsteps, heralding the arrival of Mrs Fisher herself, fatter than ever, a beaming smile lighting her homely face as she spread her plump arms to embrace her beloved Miss Cassy.

'Oh, welcome home, my dear, welcome home!' she cried as Cassy returned her hug. 'Good heavens, look how thin you are! You haven't been eating properly, have you?'

Cassy laughed. 'Of course I have, Fishy,' she promised. 'You know I never put on any weight.'

'Huh. I know those Americans—always on some faddy diet or other. Well, never mind—a bit of Fishy's good cooking inside you will do you a power of good, eh?'

'Now don't you go nagging the girl, Fisher,' chimed in Jenkins as he dropped Cassy's bag on the floor. 'She's barely stepped inside the door—you'll be driving her away again.'

'She's not going anywhere,' asserted Grandpa, taking Cassy's arm possessively. 'She's going to be staying right here, where she belongs.'

Cassy's eyes opened in surprise. 'But, Grandpa . . . I've only come down for a few weeks,' she tried to protest.

'Nonsense! You can stay as long as you like,' he insisted.

'But Grandpa, I have a job . . .'

He waved his hand dismissively. 'Oh, we can talk about that later,' he declared. 'I need to sit down. I'm not so young, you know, to be driving all that way.'

Cassy sighed. 'I told you not to overtire yourself. Do you want to go up to your room?'

'No, no, my chair will do.' He leaned heavily on her arm as she helped him into his comfortable sitting-room overlooking the back garden, and settled him into his old armchair by the fireplace. She frowned down at him anxiously. He had seemed so well just a moment before. Maybe she really should think about coming home for good.

CHAPTER TWO

BUT by dinner time, Grandpa seemed perfectly
recovered. He chattered away happily, bringing her
up to date with all the latest local gossip. 'You
remember the Liddles—the ones that used to have
the newsagents, before those Devon people took it
over.'

'Grandpa,' she interrupted him gently, 'you've
told me that story before.'

He looked surprised. 'Have I?'

'Yes. And besides, it's time we had a proper
talk.' A wary look came into his eyes. 'I really was
worried when I read that letter. You made it sound
as if something was wrong, but now I'm here
everything seems perfectly all right.'

He lifted his hand to brush away an imaginary
tear in that familar gesture. 'Does there have to be
something wrong before you'll come and visit your
poor old Grandpa?' he asked plaintively.

She leaned forward and squeezed his hand. 'Of
course not. But if there *is* something wrong, I just
wish you'd tell me.'

He managed a brave smile. 'Oh, it's nothing for
my little blue-eyed girl to worry about.'

'Grandpa, I'm not a kid any more—I'm too old
for your fairy-stories. Is it money? Have you had a
big loss on the horses?'

He looked a little put out by her bluntness.
'Certainly not!' he protested in righteous indig-

nation. 'I admit that I occasionally indulge myself with a little wager . . .'

'Then what is it?' she asked seriously.

He hesitated for a moment, but then his shoulders seemed to sag as he conceded defeat. 'I'm going to lose the house,' he admitted reluctantly. 'I'm being evicted.'

Cassy stared at him across the dinner-table. *This* house? But . . . Grandpa, how can you? You own it, don't you?'

He shook his head sadly. 'I only had it on a lease—and it expires next month.'

She stared at him in horror. Lose the house . . . No—it wasn't possible! Tears sprang to her eyes as a hundred memories flooded into her mind. And for Grandpa it must be even worse. 'Oh, Grandpa!' She jumped up, and ran to him, kneeling on the floor beside him and wrapping her arms around him.

He stroked his hand over her hair. 'I don't mind so much for myself,' he said. 'I can always go into a home. But what about Fisher and Jenkins?'

'But . . . they can't just throw you out on the street,' she protested. 'Aren't there laws to protect your rights?'

'I've checked it with my solicitor. There's nothing I can do—I just can't afford the price they're asking for the freehold.'

'How much would you need?'

'At least a hundred and twenty thousand.'

She bit her lip. 'Oh . . . Well, so much for my first idea—I could never get a mortgage that big. Would they renew the lease?'

'I made enquiries. Neither the bank nor the building society would lend money on it for anything but a long-term lease—and then you're talking about a lot of money again.'

She looked up into his tired old face. He shouldn't have to face all this, not at his time of life. He needed a little peace and security. 'There really *must* be something we can do,' she insisted.

'Now, now—don't you worry your pretty little head about it. Grandpa will sort everything out.'

She laughed, shaking her head. 'Grandpa, no fairy-stories, remember? I'm twenty-four years old. We'll sort it out together. Maybe the owner would be prepared to let you stay here, and just pay rent?' He was shaking his head again. 'But surely . . . he *can't* just throw you out. Maybe we could negotiate something.'

'Negotiate?' He drew himself up with magnificent hauteur. 'With James Clayton? Never!'

Cassy stared at him in shock. '*He* owns this house?' she demanded.

'Well, of course. Who else would it be? I took it from his grandfather on a fifty-year lease. Only for your dear grandmother's sake, mind—I'd have had nothing from Clayton, but she wanted to stay here in the village. Well, it was natural—she'd grown up here, all her friends were here. So I swallowed my pride. Oh, my dearest Elizabeth.' He lifted his tired old eyes as if to heaven. 'I'm just glad she isn't here to see this—it would break her heart.'

She hugged him fiercely. 'Don't get upset, Grandpa. Remember what you've always told me? When you have a run of bad luck, that's when you have to hang on—the luck always turns in the end.'

Her words seemed to revive his spirits. 'That's right,' he declared, his eyes sparkling. 'We won't let the damned Claytons get one over on the Durwards, will we? Something will turn up—it always does. You stick by your old Grandpa, and we'll be all right.'

'Of course.' He had always humoured her, promised her that everything would be all right—and in the small world of her childhood, he had usually been able to arrange that it was. But now the roles had been reversed—it was up to her to find a way to sort this problem out. 'Anyway, there's no point worrying about it tonight. Come on, what about a game of chess?'

Grandpa kept early hours, and it was barely ten o'clock when Cassy went up to her room—the room she had had ever since she was a child. It was all so comfortably familiar—even the pink and white counterpane on the bed still had the tiny rip in it that Mr Tibbs, the fat old cat who now stalked the kitchen regions, had torn with his claw when he had been a playful kitten.

And now James Clayton was going to take it all away. Her fist clenched tightly in anger. Though the cost of the freehold was a fortune to them, it must be almost pocket-money to him—he was a multi-millionaire. And that fortune had been made with the help of the Durwards—a help that had been repaid by a callous swindle. It was a story she had know since she was a child.

The Claytons had been tenant-farmers on Durward land for generations, with acres of orchards and market-garden. The two families had been friendly. Grandpa had often told her how he used to go fishing with Giles Clayton. Giles's father had even borrowed money from Grandpa's father to start a canning factory. It had been a good time to get into tinned food—the factory had prospered.

But for Grandpa, things had been different. His father had died when he was just twelve, and the trustees that had been appointed to guard his inheritance had had little idea of investment. By the time he came of age, death duties and inflation had taken a heavy toll. He had done his best to repair the damage, but in order to raise the capital he had needed he had had to take out mortgages on some of his land—and Bradley Park.

And who better to trust than his own brother-in-law? He was the last person he would have thought would cheat him. But Giles Clayton had become greedy. He had forged Grandpa's signature on some papers—Cassy didn't quite understand all the details. Grandpa had never been able to prove it. But he had lost virtually everything; and his young wife, never able to recover from her brother's betrayal, had finally killed herself—she had thrown herself from the high Clifton Suspension Bridge at Bristol.

And now James Clayton was going to throw him out on the street. Well, not if she could do anything about it, Cassy vowed fiercely. If she could get her hands on those forged papers . . . Maybe she wouldn't be able to prove anything, but at least she would be able to threaten to embarrass him with a nasty scandal, bad publicity—enough to make him leave Grandpa in peace for the last years of his life.

She sat down on the padded window-seat, hugging her knees and gazing pensively out over Grandpa's overgrown garden and down the valley beyond. It was a clear, cold, moon-bright night, and the lights of the village twinkled back to the stars in the black sky high above. All was quiet—in this peaceful part of the world, people rarely stirred from their own hearths after dark. Down in the village some of the farm-workers might still be gathered at the bar of the Rose and Crown, but up here only foxes and badgers were abroad.

Her eyes strayed on up the hill, to where the dark trees surrounding the Big House cut off the light of the stars. It made her so angry to think of James Clayton sitting up there in comfort and luxury, while poor Grandpa was worrying himself frantic at the prospect of losing his home.

Suddenly a crazy idea sprang into her mind. Her first reaction was to dismiss it out of hand, but obstinately it came back, and challenged her to think of something better. At least it was worth a try . . . After all, she *did* know the layout of the grounds . . . She glanced at her watch. It was too early yet—she would have to wait an hour or so.

While she was waiting, she changed into a faded pair of jeans and a jumper that she found in the bottom of her wardrobe, and as an afterthought tucked her hair up into an old woollen hat, so that even if she were spotted she wouldn't be recognised. Tiptoeing downstairs, she let herself out into the garden.

Her heart was pounding with excitement as she hurried up the path to the high, forbidding wall of Bradley Park. The ivy that hung over the gate hadn't been disturbed for years. The hinges were rusty, and creaked complainingly as she pushed it open—but it was some distance from the house, and the sound would be muffled by the trees. The moonlight filtered brightly through the canopy of leaves, helping her pick out the half-forgotten path through the tangled undergrowth.

The north-east corner of the house stood about twenty yards back from the trees, but no light showed in the tall windows. Emboldened, Cassy crept forward and peered into the first room. Though it was in darkness, she knew that it was the library. But she wasn't going to be able to get in that way; through the glass she could see the thin line of a wire running down the wall—the burglar alarm.

Silently she moved around to the back of the house, facing south over the valley. Here a wide terrace of neatly manicured lawns and gravel paths led down to a small ornamental lake, silver in the tranquil moonlight. A chink of light spilled from between curtains just a few feet away from her. With infinite caution she crept up to the French window, and peered in. She could just see James's dark head against the wing of a large leather armchair. He was watching a snooker tournament on the television.

The room was a small drawing-room, apparently for the use of the man of the house. The curtains were a rich chestnut-coloured velvet that toned with the tobacco shades of the carpet. The room was lit by several graceful Art Deco lamps, and on the classic marble mantelshelf was a beautiful antique clock. She had seen one similar at auction a few months ago—a Pierre Lianne, made in Geneva . . .

Suddenly the night erupted in the barking of dogs. Two sleek silver-grey Weimaraners had leapt up from James's feet and launched themselves furiously at the window. Cassy had a fleeting glimpse of James's face as he turned to the window, and then she was off and running for the shelter of the trees.

Behind her she heard the window open, setting off the jangle of a burglar alarm, and an angry shout called on her to stop, but she was already under the first branches. The dogs were at her heels, but in the dense undergrowth she almost escaped. She had almost reached the gate when he brought her down with a rugby tackle worthy of Twickenham.

She struggled wildly, but it was no use. Her struggles availed only to reveal to her captor that it was the soft roundness of a female body he held in his arms, not the skinny youth he had expected. With an exclamation of astonishment he forced her on to her back, pinning both her wrists to the ground beside her shoulders.

Her hat had fallen off in her flight, and her hair spilled over her shoulders, gleaming silvery blonde in the moonlight. He couldn't fail to recognise her. A mocking smile curved his hard mouth as he looked down at her. 'Well, well. Good evening, my dear,' he taunted. 'This is a pleasant surprise.'

She tried once more to squirm free, but he was far too strong for her. She was trapped beneath his weight, and the glint in his dark eyes told her that he was deriving considerable enjoyment from every movement of her body, so she lay still. She was panting for breath, and her heart was pounding as she gazed up into his face.

'That's better,' he approved as he sensed her surrender. The two dogs settled themselves on the ground, watchful guardians. James surveyed her with satisfaction. 'I didn't know that burglars could be so pretty,' he drawled with sardonic humour. 'It could almost be a pleasure to be robbed.'

'Don't be ridiculous,' she retorted sharply. 'You know full well that I'm not a burglar.'

'No?' he queried in icy cynicism. 'What are you then? A spy?'

In spite of the circumstances, she could not suppress a gurgle of laughter. 'Oh yes,' she giggled. 'I'm Olga from the Volga, and I've come for the plans of the missiles.'

To her relief, that made him laugh. 'Very well then, young lady, what *are* you doing here?' he asked in a tone of civil politeness.

'I . . . I just wanted to look at the house,' she temporised. 'I often used to come in here when I was little. I wondered if anything had changed, that's all.'

He shook his head. 'Not a very plausible story. But I have to admit that it's no more implausible than that the granddaughter of the twelfth Viscount Bradley should have been reduced to burglary or industrial espionage to earn her keep.'

'Well, then—are you going to let me go?' she demanded, hoping he wouldn't notice the nervous tremor in her voice. She was all too aware of the power of his hard body, imprisoning hers. It was dark, and they were a long way from the house . . . and it didn't take the satanic gleam in his eyes to remind her of his reputation.

He smiled slowly. 'But I don't know if I should let you go,' he demurred. 'Maybe I'm wrong—maybe you *are* a burglar, after all. Perhaps I should hand you over to the police.' Her eyes widened in horror, but the mocking smile told her that he was still tormenting her. 'On the other hand,' he went on, 'I caught you myself, on my land, so perhaps I ought to deal with you myself. Don't I have *droit de seigneur* or something?'

She fought to contain the rising tide of panic that threatened to engulf her, sure that any sign of fear would only inflame him further. 'Now you really are being ridiculous,' she snapped. 'Let me go this minute.'

He laughed, low in his throat. 'But you're such a charming burglar,' he argued, his voice deceptively soft. 'If you won't steal anything from me, perhaps I should steal something from you.'

She stared up at him helplessly as he bent towards her. His mouth brushed against hers, jolting her nerve-fibres with a heart-stopping shock. Instinctively she started to struggle again, but he wasn't going to let her escape. His mouth closed over hers, and her resistance was stillborn.

She felt the languorous sweep of his tongue, probing her defences, coaxing her lips apart, and a strange, heady excitement surged through her. She was yielding beneath the onslaught of that raw male demand, surrendering without a fight as he plundered deep into the sweet, secret corners of her mouth. When he let go of her hands, she wrapped her arms around his powerful shoulders, her body melting against his as he moulded her to his hard length.

A tide of pure feminine submissiveness was flooding her veins, and what might have happened next was beyond her power to imagine, but suddenly the sound of a police siren pierced the night. James smiled wryly down at her—he really did have an attractive smile.

'Ah, the cavalry have arrived—how inopportune. Unfortunately the burglar alarm is linked directly to the local station. It seems I'll have to let you go after all. What a pity.' Reluctantly he stood up, and pulled her to her feet. She backed away from him cautiously. 'I do hope I'll have the pleasure of meeting you again under more normal circumstances,' he went on silkily. 'I feel sure I'd like to see more of you.'

If Cassy nurtured any doubts of his true meaning, the way he coolly raked her body with his mocking eyes made his implication abundantly plain. Now that she felt herself free, she allowed herself to give vent to the tide of anger that was welling inside her.

'I can assure you the sentiment is not mutual,' she snapped and, turning on her heel, she made for the wicket-gate with as much dignity as she could muster. Behind her his laughter was soft and cynical on the night air.

By the following morning, Cassy had recovered from her nocturnal adventure. If she had slept badly, if a pair of disturbing dark eyes had intruded on her dreams, she made herself put such thoughts out of her mind as she went downstairs to have breakfast with Grandpa.

Grandpa was full of plans for the day, which included a drive into Gloucestershire to visit a friend of his who owned and trained racehorses. Why don't you come with me?' he invited casually. 'You'll enjoy it. He's got some excellent bloodstock in his stables.'

It was a lovely sunny day again. Their destination was near Cheltenham, a delightful old farmhouse of weathered brick, its rambling architecture suggesting several centuries of addition and alteration. Jenkins drove straight round to the stable-yard at the back. There were several dozen stalls, of which about half were in use. Cassy could not resist going to meet the occupants.

At the end of the row was a beautiful grey filly, young and graceful. Cassy put out her hand, and the horse graciously permitted her to stroke her nose. 'You're a lovely girl, aren't you?' she murmured softly. The horse tossed her head proudly.

'Ah! I see you've already met Durward's Lady,' came a soft Irish voice close behind her. Cassy turned sharply. A sandy-haired man in an expensive-looking sheepskin coat had approached her. He was about in his middle thirties and of medium height, with a thin, clever face and sharp grey eyes—something about him made Cassy wonder if he was a bookie. He noticed her faintly puzzled expression, and hastened to introduce himself. 'I'm Michael Farrell,' he told her. 'Welcome to my stables.'

'Oh. Thank you.' She didn't quite like the way he was looking at her—he seemed to be assessing her points, as if she were one of his racehorses. 'I'm pleased to meet you,' she added coolly, and turned back to the stall.

'She's a lovely animal, isn't she?' the man pursued, ignoring her chilly manner.

She edged slightly to one side as he came a little too close. 'I didn't know Grandpa owned any horses here,' she remarked stiffly.

'Ah now, Durward's Lady is owned by a syndicate,' he explained. 'Your Grandpa only owns one

leg, as it were.' He smiled at his own thin joke.
'But when it came to naming her—well, it seemed
like a fine name, indeed—a fine name for a fine
animal.'

She could feel his eyes resting on her again,
making her skin crawl. 'Where are the other
horses?' she asked.

'Down at the gallop. Would you care to ride on
over and take a look? I can have a cob saddled up
for you.'

Cassy hesitated. It would be nice to get on a
horse again—it was several years since she had
ridden. 'Thank you,' she agreed, inclining her head
in assent. He put his hand on her elbow, and she
froze, slanting him a warning glance. He drew back
at once, but there was a certain smugness in his
smile that she didn't like.

One of the stable-lads brought her out a nice
little chestnut mare, very sweet-tempered and
obviously used to being ridden by many strangers.
When she found an experienced rider on her back
her ears pricked up alertly.

It would have been a pleasant ride had it not
been for Michael Farrell at her side. 'Your
grandfather tells me you used to ride a good deal,'
he remarked conversationally.

'When I was younger,' she responded, not
troubling to look at him.

'Ah, yes. But you still ride well,' he approved,
subjecting her to an insolent survey. 'You've a
good seat—and nice legs, too.' She slanted him a
look of cold disdain, and urged the cob into a
canter.

That smug smile was there all afternoon. The
more haughtily she behaved towards him, the

more he smiled. They watched the string of racehorses galloping over the firm green turf, and Michael gave her a brief synopsis of their bloodlines and form. Some of them he owned himself, but most were owned by syndicates.

'D'ye take an interest in the racing game, like your grandfather?' he enquired as they trotted gently back towards the stables.

'Not particularly.'

'Ah, then you must come to a meeting with me one day. I'm sure you'd enjoy it.'

'Perhaps,' she conceded thinly, sliding down from the saddle. She went round to the horse's head, and patted her nose. 'There,' she murmured. 'Thank you for a nice ride. I'm sorry, I've nothing to give you,' she added as the horse nuzzled towards her pocket. 'If I'd known I was going to meet you, I'd have brought some sugar lumps.'

Grandpa was in his element, chatting to the stable-lads as they brushed down the sweating racehorses. Cassy smiled to herself—it was nice to see him so happy.

'Well, have you had a nice afternoon?' he asked her.

'Yes, thank you.'

'Excellent, excellent. But I'm afraid I'm going to have to drag you away now—it's time we were getting along home.'

Michael Farrell walked down to the car with them, and held open the door for her to get in. 'I'm sorry you have to be going already,' he said. 'Maybe we could have dinner one evening?'

'Thank you, but I'm only home for a short time, and I want to spend as much of it as possible with my grandfather.' She extended her hand, coolly polite. 'Good afternoon, Mr Farrell.'

Again that appraising survey, that satisfied smile. 'Good afternoon, Miss Durward. I look forward to our next meeting.'

Her smile reached nowhere near her eyes, but he didn't seem to be in the least disconcerted.

Grandpa too seemed to be blissfully unaware of the constraint in her manner. 'I'm glad you took to Michael,' he told her cosily on the way home. 'I was hoping you two would get along.'

'Really?' She was a little surprised at his words. She wouldn't have thought the trainer would be the type of person Grandpa would regard as a friend—he was usually much more discriminating. But if Grandpa enjoyed his company, she would make herself tolerate his seedy manners. After all, she wouldn't have to see much of him, even if she did decide to give up her job and come home for good.

'Another telephone call, Miss Cassy.' Jenkins' tone was solemn, but his eyes were twinkling.

Cassy glanced up from the game of chess she was playing with Grandpa. 'Who is it?' she asked.

'Mr David, I believe.'

'Oh, lovely! I won't be a minute, Grandpa,' she promised, jumping up. 'Don't go moving the pieces while I'm away!'

'As if I would!'

'You know you would,' she chided him affectionately. 'Thank you, Jenkins.' She hurried out into the hall, and picked up the telephone. 'David? Hello, how are you? It's marvellous to hear from you.'

'How's New York?'

She laughed. 'Oh, very quiet,' she responded, tongue in cheek.

'How long are you staying in England?' he asked.

'I'm not sure. I think I might be back for good.'

'Really? That's great! Listen, what are you doing tomorrow night?'

Cassy hesitated. Word had got around very quickly that she was home, and she had had several invitations from old friends. She had turned most of them down—after all, she had come home to be with Grandpa. But David *had* always been one of her favourite boyfriends when she was in her teens.

'Fancy coming to a party?' David went on. 'Nothing too formal, and you should know most of the people there. Up at the Big House.'

The Big House! Her fingers tightened around the receiver. She'd been trying to think of a way to get in there to search for those forged papers, and here it was being handed to her on a plate! 'Oh . . . yes,' she said, hoping David wouldn't notice the tremor of excitement in her voice. 'I'd love to come. Thank you, David.'

'Great! I'll pick you up about half-eight, OK?'

'Fine.'

She put the receiver back in its cradle, and stood staring at it. The perfect opportunity! Any scruples she might have had about snooping in a house where she was a guest were easily dismissed. James Clayton was a cheat and a thief. If she had to stoop to underhand methods to get justice, so be it—it served him right!

'Cassy! You look sensational!'

Cassy laughed as she walked down the stairs. 'So do you. I'm glad I decided not to believe you when you said "nothing too formal".' David was looking extremely smart in an immaculate black dinner-jacket. He was a handsome young man, tall and fair, and she was glad to have him as her escort when she went into the lion's den.

Fortunately she had brought one evening dress with her, for just such an eventuality as this. It was one of her favourites, a sleek black number in a simple, sensational style. She had bought it in the same useful little shop as the navy blue linen suit. It was by a top couturier, and was so fluidly cut that the silky fabric clung and moved as she walked with a grace that was almost feline. The neckline plunged deeply at the back, baring the long curve of her spine, but the front was a little more discreet, offering just a tantalising glimpse of the soft shadow between her breasts.

She had combed her hair into an elegant style, coiling it back from her temples and catching it with hidden clips on the crown of her head, so that it fell in a shining cascade of curls down her back. She wore little jewellery—just a thin gold serpentine chain at her throat, and tiny studs in her ears.

David smiled proudly as he led her out to his car. 'Everyone's going to be jealous of me tonight,' he told her confidently. 'You'll put all the other women in the shade.'

It was only a short distance round to the massive wrought-iron gates of Bradley Park. The rhododendrons that lined the first part of the drive were in full bloom, glowing splashes of pink and mauve in the soft twilight beneath the trees. And then the trees vanished, except for the occasional gnarled oak dotted across the wide green lawns, and they had a clear view of the house. Cassy gazed at it in wonder. It really was the most beautiful house she had ever seen.

The original square block in the centre had been flanked by perfectly symmetrical wings in the late eighteenth century. The whole building, except the servants' quarters and the stables to the west, had been faced with the local mellow grey stone, and the doorway framed by a gracefully restrained Grecian portico.

The tyres crunched on the gravel of the carriage-sweep as they parked next to a long row of luxury cars. David came round to open her door, and she rested her hand lightly on his arm as they climbed the wide steps to the open front door.

CHAPTER THREE

IT WAS the first time that Cassy had—
legitimately— seen the inside of the house, and she
couldn't help gazing around her. The hall was
classically proportioned. The floor was of marble,
intricately inlaid in a medallion pattern. Fine
plaster scrollwork panelled the walls, and a
graceful chandelier of sparkling cut glass hung on a
heavy chain from the high coved ceiling.

The young butler welcomed them as correctly as
ever Jenkins would, inviting them to step through
to the main drawing-room. Cassy paused in the
doorway, looking around her in fascination. It was
a truly magnificent room, fully fifty feet long. It
occupied the main part of the original building;
when the wings had been added, this room had
been extended by the addition of a wide semi-
circular bay of french windows, overlooking the
terrace and the lake.

The lofty ceiling was gently coved, and
intricately embellished with plasterwork, cleverly
incorporating the Durward crest among the scrolls
and vine-leaves of the design. The elegant chimney-
piece was of white marble with touches of ormolu,
and above it a massive mirror in a carved and
gilded frame reflected the light of the wall-sconces
around the room.

Cassy recognised several valuable paintings on
the walls, but one in particular caught her eye. It

was a portrait of a gentleman in a black periwig and lace cravat; the jaunty feather in his hat proclaimed him a cavalier, but the face was Grandpa's to a millimetre. One of her Durward ancestors—maybe even the first viscount!

Suddenly the sound of a familiar voice cut across her thoughts. James hadn't noticed her arrival—he was still half turned away, talking to someone else, and for a moment she was able to study him privately. He was slightly taller than most of the other men in the room, and though he wore the same sort of clothes as everyone else—formal black dinner-jacket, white bow-tie—somehow that seemed only to underline a subtle difference that Cassy couldn't quite define.

It wasn't that he looked out of place; far from it—he had an air of cool self-assurance that merely wearing the right uniform could never bestow. No, it was something that lay behind that urbane façade . . . something almost dangerous.

David took her arm again, and drew her inexorably forward. James glanced up at their approach, and his eyes lit with surprise as he saw her.

'I don't suppose I need to introduce you two to each other,' said David innocently.

'Not at all,' James responded with that sorcerer's smile. He offered her his hand, impeccably polite. 'Good evening, Miss Durward.'

In the electric silence that followed, Cassy felt herself the cynosure of all eyes. Everyone in the room seemed to have sensed the sudden tension in the air, and turned to see what was happening. She held herself stiffly erect, though her heart was pounding so fast she felt faint. All she could think of was the way he had kissed her. As she lost herself in the depths of those dark eyes, it seemed as though he was going to do it again.

Reluctantly she placed her trembling fingers in his. 'Good evening, Sir James.'

A shimmer of heat ran through her at the touch of his strong fingers. He seemed to be holding her captive. 'I didn't expect that you would grant my wish so soon,' he murmured. His eyes were black as sin, drifting down lazily over her slender curves, as if he too were recalling every detail of their previous meeting. He was still holding her hand, and a strange warmth was spreading up her arm, numbing her brain. It was as if she were caught in a dream.

'Well . . . er . . . how about a drink, Cassy?' interrupted David, a measure of annoyance in his voice. The spell was broken. James let go of her hand, and Cassy felt herself quivering with reaction as David drew her away. He glanced down at her, a frown marring his handsome face. 'What was that all about?' he asked.

Cassy returned him a look of innocent enquiry. 'What was what all about?'

'You and Clayton. I didn't know you knew him that well.'

She shrugged her slim shoulders to convey indifference. 'Oh, the Claytons and the Durwards have never got on,' she explained lightly. 'It's a long-standing family feud.'

'A family feud? You could have fooled me,' he commented dubiously.

She was saved from the necessity of replying by an old friend who caught her arm. 'Cassy! I haven't seen you for ages! What have you been doing with yourself?'

It was a lively party, and Cassy was soon enjoying

herself. Many of the guests were old friends, and it was nice to chat, catching up on all the local gossip. But all the time she was aware of James on the edge of her field of vision, flirting with a succession of beautiful women. She found herself watching to see if he stayed longer with any one in particular, seemed more interested in one.

As the evening wore on, some people began to drift out through the open French windows on to the terrace. The full moon shone like a sheet of silver on the ornamental lake, where two fine swans sailed majestically past the tall reed-beds that lined the banks. It was a spellbinding scene. Almost unconsciously Cassy moved away from the gossiping group, sipping her champagne as she stood alone at the water's edge. She sensed without looking round that it was James who came to stand beside her.

'Welcome to Bradley Park,' he murmured, a trace of sardonic humour in his voice. 'I'm glad you decided to visit it again—if a little more conventionally this time.'

She kept her gaze on the swans, who had left the shelter of the reeds and were moving slowly out across the lake. 'It . . . it's a beautiful house,' she managed to say.

'Yes, it is. Your ancestors had very good taste.'

She slanted him a cool glance. 'I see there's a portrait of one of them in the drawing-room,' she remarked.

'Oh, yes. The first viscount. Something of a rogue. I believe.' His dark eyes were teasing her. 'He started life as a foot-soldier, and charmed his way into the friendship of Charles II, who gave him the title and a rich bride.'

'You seem to know a great deal about my family,'

she commented drily.

'Naturally. I take a great interest in the history of my house.'

He was deliberately provoking her, and it took a conscious effort of will not to rise to the bait. Instead she allowed a cool smile to curve her delicate mouth. 'Indeed?' she purred, injecting her voice with icy sarcasm. 'What a pity you can't erase the Durward crest from the decorations, and put in your own. What would it be, I wonder? A fork and a tin-opener?'

He laughed softly. 'What splendid arrogance!' he taunted. 'You're a Durward to the bone, my dear.'

'And proud of it,' she responded, and turning him an aloof shoulder she moved away.

The evening was passing all too quickly. Cassy hadn't forgotten her ulterior purpose, but it wasn't easy to find an opportunity to slip away and explore on her own. David was constantly at her side, and she was surrounded by friends. She sipped sparingly the crisp champagne that was flowing freely, and joined in the lively conversation, her smile a mask to hide all her emotions.

At last the long-case clock in the 'small' drawing-room struck midnight. Some of the guests were already drifting away, but many remained, and the billiard-room next to the main drawing-room had become the focus of attention.

'Mind if we go in and watch the game?' asked David as they passed the open door.

'Of course not,' agreed Cassy, feigning indifference. James was at the table. He had discarded his jacket and tie, and the top button of his shirt was unfastened, revealing a glimpse of the fine dark hair that curled at the base of his throat. He had turned his shirt cuffs back over his strong wrists, and as he strolled round the table, his cue and a cigar in one hand and a large tumbler of Scotch in the other, studying the lie of the balls with an expert eye, he looked like some rakish pool-hall king.

Cassy tried to melt back into the shadows, away from the pool of light that flooded the green baize table, but she couldn't take her eyes off him. He had put down his glass, and clamped his cigar between his teeth as he bent to line up for his shot.

She didn't really understand the rules of the game, but she was impressed by the way he doubled the red ball off the cushion and into the corner pocket, bringing a murmur of approval from the audience. He glanced up, and caught Cassy's eye across the room, and flashed her a demonic grin around the cigar. She looked away quickly. Damn the man. He *knew* the effect he had on her, and it seemed to amuse him.

It was a tense game, absorbing everyone's interest. She couldn't hope for a better opportunity to search the house. David barely spared her a nod when she murmured to him to excuse her for a few moments. The door behind her stood slightly ajar, and like a shadow she melted through it.

She was in the corridor that ran through the east wing of the house. She stood for a moment, trying to get her bearings. To her right was the small sitting-room where she had seen James on her previous visit, to her left the hall. James's office was off the hall, but there were several people at that end of the corridor. There could be another way into the room through the library, which was opposite her. Very quietly she pushed open the door.

There was no one in there. She turned on the light, closed the door carefully behind her, and looked around. It was a long room, and the walls were lined from floor to ceiling with books—the exotic, spicy smell of their leather bindings filled the air. There was an atmosphere of quiet in here broken only by the ticking of the clock. Two comfortable Edwardian library chairs, upholstered in dark green hide, stood before the fireplace, and a pair of pale green Chinese carpets covered the gleaming parquet floor.

Sure enough, there was another door that would lead into the office. She crept across the room, and turned the handle. It was locked. Cursing softly, she stepped back. That was typical—what a suspicious mind he must have! She moved quietly back to the door that led into the corridor, but as she was about to open it she heard voices outside. She would have to wait just a minute—she didn't want to bump into anyone.

She glanced around the room again. As well as books, it held several displays of fine porcelain. There was a pair of rather gaudy clown-musicians that she guessed were modelled by Kaendler at the Meissen factory, and a small boy with his dog, and an almost comic Chinese magot, modelled by someone who had never seen a real Chinaman. But the piece that caught her eye was a graceful representation of a slender young girl, draped only in a wisp of fabric, her eyes innocently downcast.

It was of biscuit-fired porcelain, as fragile as eggshells, and the delicacy of the modelling suggested Falconet. And yet . . . She picked it up carefully, and turned it over. Yes, there in the base was the impressed mark of the Sèvres factory. And yet . . .

'Well, well. Olga from the Volga, I presume?'

She spun round, almost dropping the figure.
James had come silently into the room. He closed
the door behind him, smiling at her in mocking
amusement. But there was a cold glint in his eyes
that made her shiver.

'Forgive me,' he added, subjecting her to a lazy
survey that made her suddenly acutely aware of the
way her dress clung to the slender curves of her
body, 'but where were you planning to hide that? I
can't help thinking it might be a little difficult to
conceal under that dress.'

Her heart was pounding with shock, as if she
really had been caught red-handed in the act of
stealing, but she tilted her chin in haughty
defiance. 'I told you before,' she protested, only a
slight tremor of nervousness in her voice, 'I am not
a thief.'

'No?'

The sneer in his voice turned her panic to anger.
'And if I were,' she retaliated disdainfully, 'I
certainly wouldn't trouble to steal a fake.'

He reacted with gratifying astonishment to her
words. 'A fake? You mean that Sèvres figure?'

'It isn't Sèvres,' she asserted handing it to him.
'It's a very good copy.

He turned the figure over in is hand. 'How do
you know?'

She hesitated, seeking the reasons for her
instinctive reaction. 'The modelling is of a very
high standard—I would guess it's by Falconet. But
it's in hard-paste porcelain, and the Sèvres factory
didn't use hard-paste until 1769. Falconet left
France in 1766.'

He frowned, but he didn't instantly dismiss her opinion. 'You know your antiques,' he mused.

'I like to think so.'

'And if I told you that this has been authenticated by the best experts?'

She hesitated for the briefest moment. 'I would say . . . that perhaps they were having an off-day.'

He laughed—a deep, warm laugh that she had to admit was very attractive. 'It wouldn't be the first time. I bought it at a small country auction several years ago, and just took the catalogue's word for it that it was genuine. Perhaps I should take it up to Sotheby's. Is there anything else here that you'd like to cast doubt upon? This, for instance?' He picked up the ugly magot. 'Ch'ien Lung, would you say?'

She slanted him a glance of quizzical amusement. 'Are you testing me? The nearest that's ever been to China is Chelsea.' She took the piece from him, and turned it over. 'There.' She pointed in triumph to the red anchor mark on its base.

'Very good,' he approved mockingly. 'Why did you come in here?' His tone was still light, but there was a thread of steel in it that was unmistakable.

She felt a faint blush rise to her cheeks. 'I'm sorry. I wanted a moment's quiet from the party, and I just couldn't resist exploring,' she explained, hoping he wouldn't notice the tremor in her voice.

'Then please allow me to escort you,' he returned smoothly.

Her eyes flashed with indignation. 'You still think I'm going to try to steal something?' she demanded.

'I'm not sure.' He regarded her in sardonic enquiry. 'Are you?'

'How many times do I have to tell you that I am not a thief? Would you like me to present you with personal references?'

He smiled that attractive smile again. 'I don't think that will be necessary. Come, you've started your tour in one of the best rooms. Have you had a look at the Chinese cabinet?'

She hovered on the brink of returning him a sharp answer and going back to David, but this was a perfect opportunity to have a good look around the house, without arousing suspicion. Besides, she was fascinated by the cabinet—behind the glossy laquered doors there were often dozens of intricate little drawers, many of them with secret compartments.

So she followed him down to the far end of the room. The cabinet really was a beautiful piece. The doors were elaborately decorated with images of clouds and dragons on a black ground, and inside the drawers fitted together like a Chinese puzzle.

'It's lovely,' she breathed almost reverently, leaning close to admire the incredibly skilful workmanship.

'What age would you put on it?' he challenged.

'Oh, heavens . . . I've no idea. Maybe . . . about 1780?'

'Very good. It's 1770.'

'It must be very rare,' she speculated.

'Extremely. I was very lucky to get it. I was trying to get my hands on an Italian walnut bureau at the time. I just missed out on that one, but then I heard the whisper that this was coming on the market, and I managed to get in first.'

She gazed around the room. 'You have some lovely pieces,' she commented, a tinge of envy in her voice.

'Yes. I'm rather a collector of beautiful things . . .'

Suddenly Cassy felt her heartbeat accelerating oddly—he was looking at her again with those hypnotic dark eyes, and she felt as if he were holding her captive. Suddenly, foolishly, she remembered the silly day-dreams she used to weave as a child—the Fairy Princess and the Wicked Baron.

His fingers trailed slowly up her arm. '. . . such as yourself.'

'I . . . I'm not a collector's item,' she protested, her voice a tremulous whisper.

He laid his hand along her cheek, and turned her face up towards him. 'But you're very beautiful,' he murmured.

His hand slid round to cage her skull, and drew her inexorably towards him. He bent his head, and she felt the warmth of his breath fanning her cheek. She stared up at him in a kind of fascination. His jaw had a slight sandpaper rasp, although he was cleanshaven, and his lips were firm against hers. And he really was going to kiss her again.

His mouth closed over hers, warm and enticing, inciting her to respond, and she could summon not an ounce of resistance. His tongue swirled languorously deep into the secret corners of her mouth, making her feel giddy, and she had to reach up her hands to grip his powerful shoulders to save herself from falling.

His hands slid slowly down over her bare back, curving her supple body intimately against his hard length. Heat shimmered through her, melting her bones. Strange longings were stirring inside her. This was something quite beyond her experience, and she didn't know how to stop him as he caressed her body with slow, warm sensuality.

Her head tipped back into the crook of his arm, and she could hear the ragged sound of her own breathing. He was wrapping her up, subduing her will. She had forgotten all about the party guests gathered in the next room. A shudder of pure pleasure ran through her as the hot tip of his tongue began to explore the delicate shell of her ear, and his long, sensitive fingers rose to fondle the ripe swell of her breast. Her head was dizzy with the racing of her blood, and she whispered his name on a sobbing breath.

He lifted his head for a moment, and looked down into her misted eyes. 'Very beautiful . . .' he murmured smokily.

His mouth returned to claim hers again, deep and demanding, and she yielded helplessly, her body quivering in response as his hand slipped inside her dress to caress the aching curve of her breast with secret intimacy, his clever fingers teasing the tender nipple until it puckered into an exquisitely sensitive bud. She was sinking into the languid, sensual warmth . . .

Suddenly a sharp exclamation pierced the swirling

darkness in her brain. She opened startled eyes to see David standing in the doorway, his jaw taut with anger as he took in the scene. 'What the hell . . .?'

'I'm sorry David,' apologised James at once. 'But it's really your own fault, you know. If you bring such a beautiful woman to a party, you ought to keep your eye on her.'

But David was not to be so easily mollified. 'I ought to knock your teeth down your throat,' he glowered angrily.

Only by the faintest twitch of his lips did James betray his doubt that the younger man could achieve such an ambition. 'Please don't,' he begged. 'Come on, David, let's not fall out over a thing like this.'

David turned to Cassy, hurt in his eyes as he took in the crushed state of her dress and the tangled disorder of her hair. She bit her lip in shame. 'I . . . I'm sorry,' she whispered.

'I'd better take you home,' he grated furiously.

She couldn't even look at James as David took her arm and hustled her out into the corridor. Several people were still in the hall, and Cassy felt her cheeks flame scarlet as they turned to stare in undisguised curiosity. It was a relief to get to the car, because by then her legs were almost giving way. She leaned back in the seat, and closed her eyes.

'Well, I hope you're satisfied,' snapped David as he slid in beside her at the wheel. 'You've made a complete fool of me.'

She opened her eyes, and smiled at him apologetically. 'David, I really am sorry . . .'

'And with Clayton of all people! As if you didn't know his reputation. I thought you had more sense.'

'Look, I've already apologised . . .'

'You've never even let me get to first base—and yet if I hadn't caught you, you'd have been . . . Well, I don't have to spell it out.'

'No, you don't,' Cassy retorted, her patience strained almost to breaking-point. 'I've apologised for embarrassing you. But frankly, it's none of your business if I choose to let James Clayton kiss me.'

'Kiss you!' he exploded. 'He was practically making love to you! Some family feud!'

Suddenly Cassy felt very tired. 'Please, David. Let's not argue,' she begged. 'Just take me home.'

He swung the wheel viciously, making the tyres spin on the gravel of the drive. He drove home at a reckless pace, and Cassy was only too glad that it wasn't far. He drew up outside Grandpa's house, and came round to open her door, his face still dark with anger.

She offered him her hand. 'Goodnight, David. And please, forgive me for tonight. I behaved very badly towards you.'

He smiled reluctantly. 'I just don't like to see you making a fool of yourself over a man like James Clayton,' he explained gruffly. 'You're far too good to become just another one of his conquests.'

She returned the smile. 'Thank you. But you needn't worry, you know. He . . . he just caught me off guard tonight. It certainly won't happen again.'

'I hope not.' He took her hand, suddenly looking very boyish. 'May I kiss you goodnight?' he pleaded.

She nodded. He took her into his arms, and his mouth closed over hers. He kissed nicely—he must have been getting in plenty of practice since they were teenagers, she reflected with amusement. But she was in no danger of being swept away.

After a while he let her go. 'Well . . . goodnight, then.'

'Goodnight, David.'

She hurried up the garden path, searching quickly through her handbag for her key. It was a good job that Grandpa kept such early hours; everyone had gone to bed. She tiptoed upstairs to her room, anxious not to disturb anyone. Her appearance would call for explanations that she didn't feel inclined to have to make, not tonight.

Safely in her own room, she turned on the light, and stared at her reflection in the mirror. It was worse than she had imagined. Her hair was a tousle of curls around her shoulders, and her mouth had the look of soft, crushed fruit. She touched her fingertip to her lips, remembering . . .

Damn, was she going mad? She gave herself a little shake. What was she doing, indulging thoughts like that—and about James Clayton, of all people! She hadn't needed David to remind her of his reputation—she knew it only too well. And now she was likely to be the star of the latest piece of village scandal. She pressed her hands to her heated cheeks. What if it ever got back to Grandpa!

And she couldn't even justify her actions by claiming that she had had any success in finding out about those forged papers. She had achieved nothing—worse, she had aroused his suspicions. If she had kept a clear head, maybe she could have got a job with his company, and used her position to find out what she needed to know. But it was too late now.

Wearily she got out of her creased dress, and had a wash and brushed her hair. Then she pulled on her nightdress and climbed into bed. But though she was tired, she couldn't sleep. Her mind kept returning again and again to that scene in the library. Those silly fantasies of her childhood had come to life—the Fairy Princess and the Wicked Baron.

'Ah, good morning to you, Miss Durward.'

Cassy hesitated in the doorway of the breakfast-room. After a bad night's sleep, the last person she wanted to see first thing in the morning was Michael Farrell. But her innate good manners rose at once to the situation. 'Good morning, Mr Farrell. I didn't know you were here,' she said as she took her seat at the table and poured herself a glass of orange juice.

'Sure now, I came over last night, to keep your Grandpa company, since you were going out. How was your party?'

'Very nice, thank you,' she responded in a pleasant tone. 'There were a lot of old friends there that I haven't seen for a long time.'

'Ah, 'tis a fine thing indeed, to move in that sort

of social circle,' Michael remarked. 'Where's that damn butler of yours got to?' he added impatiently. 'I rang the bell five minutes ago.'

'I'm afraid we don't have a cooked breakfast on Sundays,' Cassy explained 'Jenkins and Fishy both have the morning off. Can I make you some toast?'

There was an electric toaster on the sideboard—it was so old that Grandpa always joked that Rhoda would pay a fortune for it, but it still made good toast so long as you watched carefully to make sure it didn't stick and burn the bread. She dropped a couple of slices into it, and switched it on.

'Your grandfather told me that you were a good cook,' Michael told her.

Cassy's lips twitched. 'Did he?' she enquired with dry amusement.

'In fact, he's told me a great deal about you.'

'All good, I hope?' she asked lightly.

'Of course. And now that I've met you, I find that it's all true.'

Cassy managed a thin smile. His ingratiating tone was beginning to get on her nerves—and she didn't much like the way he was looking at her, either.

'I've a great deal of regard for your grandfather,' Michael went on. 'I'm very sad to see hm in his present difficulties. I'd be very glad to help him out.'

She glanced at him in surprise—she wouldn't have expected Grandpa to have confided his financial difficulties to Michael Farrell. 'Well, thank you,' she responded uncertainly. 'But I don't think . . . that is, Grandpa wouldn't like to borrow money from a friend.'

That self-satisfied smile spread slowly across Michael's face. 'Not a friend, certainly. But if I were to be . . . one of the family.'

Cassy frowned in confusion. 'One of the family?' she repeated blankly.

'Indeed. Ah, now, I appreciate that this has come up rather suddenly, but you seem to me to be an intelligent woman. Look upon it as a business proposition, if you like.'

She stared at him in slowly dawning horror. 'W . . . what are you suggesting?' she asked carefully.

He chuckled with laughter. 'Oh, my intentions are entirely honourable, I assure you,' he declared unctuously. 'It's matrimony I have in mind.'

CHAPTER FOUR

CASSY stared at Michael Farrell in stunned disbelief. 'You think I'm going to *marry* you?' she breathed.

'Certainly. You're just the sort of wife I want—a thoroughbred, the best blood-lines.'

'You must be crazy!'

Hot anger blazed in his eyes, but he kept it under strict control. 'Not at all,' he answered smoothly. 'I'm prepared to buy you the freehold of this house as a wedding present.'

Suddenly Cassy smelled burning, and turned to see that the toaster had stuck. 'Oh!' The accident provided her with a welcome diversion. Flustering to deal with the crisis, she managed to pretend that the past few minutes hadn't happened. 'I'm sorry—I'll make you some more,' she said quickly. 'I'd better go and get some more bread. I won't be a minute.'

She made good her escape, scampering down to the empty kitchen. She was stunned by what Michael had said. *Marry* him? Surely he couldn't have meant it? He must have been joking—some people did have a pretty weird sense of humour! With an effort of will, she pulled herself together and, taking another couple of slices of bread from the pantry, she went back upstairs.

Grandpa was at the breakfast table when she walked into the room. 'Ah, Cassy, my dear,' he greeted her with a beaming smile. 'Now, what do you think? Michael has invited us to go up to Cheltenham for a few days.'

'Oh?' She cast a wary glance towards Michael, but his expression was bland. She could almost have thought she had imagined their previous conversation.

'There's a two-day meeting at Chepstow,' Grandpa went on.

'Oh, I see.' She smiled at him fondly. 'Well, you go, Grandpa. I don't think I'd really enjoy horse-racing very much.'

'How do you know until you try?' put in Michael silkily. 'Why don't you just come along?'

'No, thank you,' she repeated sharply. Grandpa caught the edginess in her voice, and looked at her in surprise. She flushed slightly, and turned her attention to the toaster. 'Now, let's see if I can manage to organise breakfast without burning the house down!'

No more was said about the visit to Michael's until after breakfast. Michael had already left—Grandpa had preferred to wait for Jenkins rather than go in Michael's car, but now he was getting impatient.

'Where's the old fool got to now?' he demanded crossly. 'It doesn't take this long to get back from church. Gossiping with the old women, I dare say.'

'Did he know you wanted him?' she asked.

'Well, he might have guessed. But I suppose it's all of a kind. No one takes a bit of notice of what I want.'

'Grandpa . . .'

'You're exactly the same,' he grumbled. 'I thought you'd come home to see me, and you won't even come to Cheltenham with me.'

'But you're only going for a couple of days,' she pointed out reasonably.

'So? You seem to forget that I'm an old man. Even a few days, at my time of life . . .'

She chuckled with laughter. 'Grandpa, if you really think you're in imminent danger of meeting your maker, do you really think you ought to be spending your last days at a racecourse?' she enquired in dry amusement.

He drew himself up indignantly. 'Well, if you can only make a joke of it . . .'

'Grandpa, you've never looked healthier. You go off and enjoy yourself. We've got plenty of time to be together.'

'We have?' A look of hope sprang to his eyes. 'You mean you're not going back to New York?'

'No.' She gave him a hug. 'I'm going to stay here. Heaven knows what I'll do for a job, but I'll think about that later—I've got a bit of savings, so I'll manage for a little while. And first thing on Monday I'll go and see the solicitor about this lease. There must be a way to sort everything out.'

'Of course there is,' he agreed, beaming happily. 'In a couple of months, we'll look back on all this and laugh.'

It was a beautiful spring day. After she had seen Grandpa off in the Rolls, with the vast quantity of luggage he deemed essential for a trip of a few days, she wandered out into the garden. Only the part nearest the house was neatly tended. The rest was quite wild, with straggling roses vying for space with self-sown pansies and wild meadow flowers, and honeysuckle running unchecked over everything.

She surveyed it grimly. While she had some time to herself, she might as well try to do something about it. She found a wheelbarrow and a pair of secateurs in the toolshed, and set to with a will.

There was something remarkably satisfying in slicing through the woody branches of the rose-bushes or dragging out great handfuls of tangled honeysuckle. It seemed to soothe the turmoil of emotions that the vivid memories of last night aroused.

She was bending over, trying to reach an awkward branch, when a lazy voice behind her remarked, 'What a delightful sight.'

She straightened, and spun round sharply to see James standing in the wicket-gate, his eyes lingering with evident approval over her slender figure. She flashed him a fulminating glare, but he returned only a taunting smile.

'I do like a natural garden,' he added in the politest conversational tone, as if to deceive her that it had not been her neat *derrière*, clad in a pair of tight faded jeans, to which he had been referring.

'Good morning, Sir James,' she said with a valiant effort to retain her composure. 'If you've come to see my grandfather, I'm afraid you've just missed him. He's gone away for a few days.'

'But I haven't come to see him,' he told her, a light touch of mockery in his voice. 'I've come to see you.'

'Oh?' It was all she could trust herself to say.

'Must you be so formal this morning?' he enquired teasingly. 'I thought that after last night . . .'

'If you were a gentleman,' retorted Cassy acidly, 'you would not refer to last night.'

'Then I am plainly not a gentleman.'

'If you were a gentleman, last night would not have happened,' she snapped, furious with herself for betraying her stormy emotions.

'Ah, but think what fun we'd have missed,' he taunted.

'That was *not* my idea of fun!'

He lifted one eyebrow in mocking enquiry. 'Oh? I rather got the impression that you were enjoying it as much as I was.'

'Well, I wasn't. And what's more, I think you're the most arrogant man I have ever met!'

'Am I really?' he returned, quite unabashed. 'I'm glad to have made such a strong impression.'

Cassy took a deep, steadying breath, fighting for self-control. She musn't let him make her lose her temper—she couldn't afford to antagonise him when he had the power to grant or refuse an extension on Grandpa's lease. She turned back to the rose-bush, and began lopping off some of the smaller branches. 'If you have come to apologise,' she said with difficulty, 'I'm more than ready to forget the whole thing.'

He laughed softly. 'Are you? I'm not—not yet. *I'd* like to do it again.'

It was difficult to think with him standing so close. She edged carefully away from him, her mind fumbling with a dozen questions. Should she bring up the subject of the lease now? No, maybe it was better to wait until she'd seen Grandpa's solicitor, and knew all the facts. He wouldn't be an easy person to negotiate with.

'Do you know, that's the third time you've trimmed that particular branch?' he enquired tauntingly.

With an effort of will she gathered the scattered threads of her composure, and lifted her eyes to meet his. 'Was there something you wanted, Sir James?' she enquired, only a slight tremor of nervousness in her voice.

'Only the pleasure of your company at dinner tonight,' he responded, turning on that fatally attractive smile.

She hesitated. Have dinner with him? It was dangerous, and yet . . . after all, what could he do to her? If she was careful, kept her head, maybe she would get a chance to find out where he kept those forged papers. Provided she kept her head.

She lowered her eyes demurely. 'You still haven't apologised for what happened last night,' she protested, deliberately coy.

'If I do, will you have dinner with me?'

'I'll consider it.'

'In that case, I apologise unreservedly,' he returned at once.

She slanted him a wary glance from beneath her lashes. There was nothing apologetic in his smile—in fact he looked as if, given the chance, he would do exactly the same thing again. Well, it was up to her to make sure he didn't get the chance.

'Apology accepted,' she murmured, a tiny smile flirting over her lips.

'Thank you. So I'll pick you up this evening. Shall we say eight o'clock?'

She nodded her assent, and he saluted her with a sardonic bow. And then he was gone, strolling away across the garden, leaving her staring at the gate as he closed it behind him. She pressed her hands to her heated cheeks. What had she done? She must have been crazy even to dream of taking a risk like that! A man with his reputation! And yet . . . if it worked . . .

It was difficult to know what to wear. She couldn't wear the black dress again—apart from anything else, it was too creased. Unexpectedly, it was Fishy who came up with the solution—she had told her that she was going out to dinner, and let her assume that it was with David.

'Why don't you see if there's anything in one of your grandmother's trunks?' she suggested. 'Those old-fashioned dresses are back in style now, aren't they? I'm sure you'd find something to suit you—you're the image of her, you know.'

'Oh, yes!' cried Cassy excitedly. 'Heavens, I haven't looked in those trunks for years. Do you remember how I used to dress up in her things when I was little? Those lovely big hats?'

'I remember,' smiled Fishy fondly. 'And I remember how you used to clump around in her shoes, that were far too big for you, until that time you fell down the attic stairs, just like I warned you you would.'

'And sprained my wrist,' Cassy remembered ruefully, 'so I couldn't go in for the Pony Club gymkhana.'

'It taught you a lesson,' Fishy chided her, just as if she were still eleven years old.

Cassy laughed. 'Well, I'm going up to look right now. Are you coming?'

Fishy shook her head. 'No. I can't manage those stairs any more. You pick something, and fetch it down to show me.'

The trunks were filled with the delicate perfume of lavender. The clothes had been packed so carefully that even after half a century in storage they were as good as new. Cassy fingered them almost reverently. There were beaded boleros and lace blouses, and chic little Chanel suits, and dresses so lovely they made her gasp in delight.

She pulled one out, and held it up against herself. It was of delicate silk crêpe de Chine, cleverly bias-cut to cling. The colour was a rich shade of sapphire-blue, and it was trimmed with a deep fall of lace, tinted to a perfect match, from knee to hem. There was a kind of long bolero of the same lace to wear with it.

Eagerly Cassy ran down the attic stairs to her own room, and stripped off her clothes to try on the dress. It fitted as if it had been made for her, and the colour was the perfect complement to the sapphire-blue of her eyes. She danced down the stairs to show it off.

'Oh! You look so like her,' sighed Fishy. 'I remember that dress so well. It's by Schiaparelli, you know. She bought it in Paris—not long after she married your grandfather. Oh, she was so lovely, so full of life. She could have had her pick. When I think . . .' She brushed a tear from the corner of her eye. 'Oh dear, hark at me running on. Go and take the dress off now, and I'll run the iron over it.'

Cassy took a long time to get ready. She lingered in her bath, her mind empty, just enjoying the sensation of the warm water caressing her soft skin. She didn't want to let herself think too much about the evening ahead—or admit to herself that she was looking forward to it rather more than her ostensible reasons for accepting the invitation warranted.

She tried several hair-styles, but eventually decided to leave her hair loose and curling around her shoulders, just catching it up over one temple with an ivory comb. Just a touch of make-up, and then the dress. She twirled before the mirror, peeping over her shoulder to catch a glimpse of the rear view. Oh, it was such a lovely dress! She could just imagine her grandmother on the night she had worn it—she would have been just the same age as Cassy.

Suddenly the sound of the doorbell sliced through her thoughts. She caught her breath. He was here! She spun round in agitation, searching frantically for her handbag, and found it on the bed, exactly where she had left it. She had to hurry—she had told Fishy not to bother to answer the door, and was desperately hoping that the plump housekeeper would be too comfortable to stir from her armchair in the kitchen.

The evil of the Claytons must be rubbing off on to her, she reflected wryly, that she should be deceiving dear Fishy like this, but she didn't want Grandpa to find out what she was up to. She had a feeling he wouldn't approve!

Her hurry brought a delicate flush to her cheeks, and the hall light behind her shone in her hair like a halo. James did not trouble to hide his approval. 'Absolutely stunning!' was his verdict.

Her heart was beating a little too fast, but she managed to retain a façade of cool composure. 'Thank you,' she returned as she stepped past him to where his chauffeur was holding open the door of an elegant champagne-coloured Rolls-Royce.

Why the display of luxury? Did he think she would be impressed? She stole a glance at him as he handed her very correctly into the car. Even in his formally elegant black dinner-jacket he exuded a raw masculinity that did strange things to her equilibrium. She was going to have to be very careful if she was to keep the situation under control.

He leaned back at his ease in the opposite corner as the car purred down the hill, his dark eyes watching her with the unnerving steadiness of a jungle cat stalking his prey. 'You know, you intrigue me,' he remarked lightly. 'I didn't expect you to come out with me tonight.'

'Oh?'

'I'd love to know what's going on behind those big beautiful eyes of yours.'

She managed to evade that mesmerising gaze. 'I . . . I don't know what you're talking about,' she murmured defensively.

'The way you blow so hot and cold. I can never

predict how you're going to react. I find it very . . . entertaining.'

'I *am* glad,' she purred, her claws drawn. 'I would hate to bore you.'

His laughter was as soft as velvet. 'Oh, I don't think you could ever do that.'

They had reached the bottom of the hill and turned over the bridge to drive through the village. Cassy felt herself tense slightly, hoping no one would recognise her—if she were seen in James's car, the gossips would have a field day, especially after what had happened last night! Her mind sought for something casual to say to turn the conversation into safer channels.

'It was a nice desk you bought in New York,' she remarked lightly. 'Where are you going to put it?'

'I've no idea,' he answered, an inflection of ironic humour in his voice. 'It just caught my eye, so I decided to have it.'

'You're very fortunate that you can afford to do that,' she returned caustically.

He laughed softly. 'I told you—I like to collect beautiful things. Even if sometimes they prove a little . . . expensive.'

She could feel herself burning in the heat of his gaze. 'And I told you,' she retorted in a tense voice, 'I've no intention of being added to your collection.'

'No? It's rather an intriguing game, don't you think, my dear? Each of us is trying to get something from the other, and trying to give nothing away. Whose strategy do you think will win?'

'I . . . I'm not playing any game,' she protested, avoiding his eyes.

'Aren't you? And yet you've come out with me tonight. Why, I wonder?'

Cassy could think of nothing to say. She turned her gaze out of the window on the darkening countryside, but she could sense him behind her, so close, his presence making her spine shiver as if it were crystallising into ice. Surely he couldn't have guessed her intentions? No, that was unlikely. But he certainly seemed to suspect her of having some underhand motive. She would have to be careful.

At last the tyres crunched on the gravel of a drive, and they drew up before a charming black and white inn, close to the river.   Cassy had a fleeting impression of mullioned windows and crenellated chimneys as the chauffeur politely held open the door for her again.

The evening air was as soft and shadowed as a dream. She was aware of James close behind her, and briefly allowed herself to savour the moment before the next move of the game compelled her forward. She advanced gracefully up the wide, shallow steps, leaving James to follow in her wake.

A liveried doorman stood at the entrance, bowing formally, and as they moved into the imposing foyer the head waiter came forward to greet them in a finely tuned blend of dignity and deference.

'Good evening, Sir James,' he said. 'We are most happy to welcome you to the Mermaid again.'

'Thank you, Claude,' replied James in a pleasant tone that would ensure that he was treated with more than mere dutiful respect. 'Are you busy tonight?'

'Fairly full, sir. I have reserved your usual table, of course. Would you care for an aperitif while you order?'

'Cassy?'

'Yes, please,' she agreed at once. Though she usually drank little, she was feeling in need of a little Dutch courage to support her through the evening. James led her into a softly lit lounge, and over to a table by one of the long windows. It looked out over the river, sparkling like a ribbon of silver beneath the full moon.

She ordered a martini, and let her eyes wander around the elegant room. The décor was dark green and bronze, and everywhere the mermaid motif was discreetly repeated—in the bronze bases of the lamps that lit the room with their soft glow, in the discreet emblem woven into the damask of the dark green table-cloths.

The head waiter brought the menu, and in the distraction of ordering from the tempting selection she could further postpone the need to make conversation. James chose a wine, and then they were left alone. She sipped her drink, watching him cautiously beneath her lashes.

'How long have you lived in New York?' he began in a conversational tone.

'Nearly six years now.'

'And do you like it?'

'I love it—most of the time,' she told him frankly. 'I do miss the countryside now and then, but my apartment is quite close to Central Park, so when I feel the need for a little greenery around me, I go for a walk.'

'Very convenient. Rhoda must pay you very well if you can afford to live in the heart of Manhattan.'

'She does,' Cassy answered coolly. She didn't bother to explain that the apartment was owned by Rhoda, and leased to her at a peppercorn rent.

'I feel responsible for you,' Rhoda had insisted. 'I don't want you coming to work on the subway and getting mugged.'

'Don't you get nervous, walking alone in Central Park?'

'Not these days—it's much better than it used to be, you know.'

'Maybe next time I'm over there, you could take me sightseeing—if you can spare half a day from your busy schedule,' he suggested, those black-magic eyes hinting that he wasn't really interested in the World Trade Centre.

'I . . . I don't think I'm going back,' she stammered defensively.

'Oh?' He raised an enquiring eyebrow. 'I got the impression that you were only over here for a short holiday.'

'I was, initially. But . . . I've changed my mind. My grandfather is not getting any younger—he needs me to look after him.'

'So you're giving up your career, and your Manhattan apartment?'

There was a faint note of scepticism in his voice, and her eyes flashed coldly. 'Of course. I'm the only family he's got.' She was beginning to find the conversation difficult to handle, and she was more than grateful for the interruption of the head waiter, returning to invite them to their table.

The restaurant was almost full, but they had the best table, close to the white-suited pianist who was playing quietly to entertain the diners. James helped her to her seat, and sat down opposite her, all formal politeness as the efficient waiters served their meal.

It was a relief to be able to focus all her attention on her plate. The food was superb. The lamb was tender and succulent, and the wine James had chosen was the perfect complement to it—a fine, clear Médoc, with a delicately herbal bouquet.

'That was excellent,' she approved as the waiter came to remove the plates.

James smiles. 'More wine?'

'A little, thank you.' She glanced at the label on the bottle. It was one that Craig had been trying to buy in bulk to import into the States.

He lifted a faintly mocking eyebrow. 'Are you an expert on wine, as well as antiques?' he enquired.

'Enough to appreciate a good Chateau Margaux,' she responded with dignity.

He sat back in his seat, regarding her over the rim of his glass. 'Rhoda really must have been paying you well,' he commented drily. 'You've managed to cultivate some very expensive tastes—a Manhattan apartment, the best wines, couture clothes—oh, I've had my cheque-book out in enough Bond Street establishments to recognise the cut. How on earth are you going to manage if you give up your job?'

She returned him a frosty look. 'I'll manage.'

'I'm sure you will.'

There was a note of chilling cynicism in his voice which puzzled her. 'What do you mean by that?' she asked him.

His smile mocked her. 'Don't play the ingenue with me, Cassy. I didn't come down with the last shower of rain. I think you and I could do very well together. We have a great deal in common.'

'Oh?'

'We share a liking for the good things in life—French food, fine porcelain, making love . . .'

His voice was as warm and mellow as the rich wine, and it was all she could do to avoid the mesmerising darkness of his gaze. Summoning every ounce of poise at her disposal she leaned back in her seat, and took a delicate sip of her wine.

'But too much French food would be fattening,' she responded, matching his tone of sardonic amusement. 'And I can only afford to indulge myself at auctions on behalf of Rhoda. And as for making love—I really wouldn't know. I've never tried it.'

His eyebrows shot up in undisguised astonishment. 'Never?'

She could feel a slow blush rising from her throat. Why on earth had she let that slip? 'No doubt it comes as a surprise to you to learn that some girls set too much value on themselves to jump into bed the first time you take them out to dinner,' she retorted coldly.

'Indeed?' His hard mouth curved into a mocking smile. 'Well then, since everything has its price—it's your words I'm quoting—what value do you set on your favours, Miss Durward?'

His meaning was unmistakable, and her eyes flashed blue flame. 'I *beg* your pardon?' she demanded in a voice that would strip paint.

'Or are you holding out for the highest bid?' he persisted provocatively. 'A wedding ring, perhaps?'

'What's wrong with that?' she returned with cold

disdain.

He shook his head. 'What a pity,' he murmured. 'I'm not prepared to bid that far. I don't supose you'd be prepared to negotiate?'

Her hand was shaking so much that she had to put her glass down. 'Negotiate?' she repeated, the significance of his words chilling her.

'Certainly,' he responded smoothly. 'I've no intention of marrying you, but that doesn't mean I'm not interested in what's on offer.'

Cassy had to fight to suppress the tide of anger that was seething inside her. 'You . . . you want me to be your *mistress?*' she demanded, stunned.

That fatally attractive smile curved his hard mouth. 'Mistress—what a delightfully old-fashioned word for it,' he taunted softly. 'But I like it. So, yes, I want you to be my mistress.' His dark eyes were caressing her, making her skin flame as if he were touching her. 'I've rarely met a woman who responds the way you do. I would very much like to continue where we left off.'

Unconsciously she reached for her wine-glass again, but her hand knocked against it, and the red stain spilled across the pristine table-cloth. She stared at it, trembling with reaction.

'It's nothing,' James reassured her quickly, discreetly summoning the waiter to deal with the accident. 'Shall we go now?'

'Oh . . . oh, yes . . .' she stammered, rising to her feet and allowing him to draw her hand through his arm and lead her through the crowded restaurant.

The head waiter hurried forward to bid them farewell. 'I trust you have enjoyed your evening?' he enquired solicitously.

'Very much,' responded James smoothly.

'Excellent. I look forward to welcoming you again, Sir James. And the lovely lady, of course.' He bowed over her hand with Gallic charm, and Cassy managed a faint smile as James drew her out into the lofty entrance hall. She slanted a wary glance up at him, and he lifted one eyebrow in sardonic amusement.

'What's wrong?' he enquired tauntingly. 'Afraid I'm going to try to seduce you on the way home?' Her cheeks suffused with colour, and he laughed softly. 'Oh no, my dear. You need have no fear on that score,' he mocked. 'Contrary to the notions of some romantic novelists, the back of a Rolls-Royce is not exactly the ideal setting. I shall save the pleasure for a more suitable occasion.'

'There isn't going to be one,' she vowed.

'No? We shall see.'

'Don't hold your breath,' she advised him caustically.

He burst out laughing. 'Do you know, I like you best when you let that ladylike façade slip a little, and the spitfire underneath shows through,' he taunted. 'I've a feeling you're going to be great in bed.'

CHAPTER FIVE

JAMES'S behaviour was impeccable on the way home—he really had no choice, with Greening at the wheel. But as he bid her goodnight, kissing her hand with mocking formality, his dark eyes met hers. 'Thank you for a most delightful evening,' he murmured. 'I shall certainly look forward to our next meeting.'

Cassy couldn't answer. Snatching her hand away, she ran up the garden path, and let herself into the quiet house, grateful that there was no one to see her pale face. She ran up to her room, and closed the door, leaning against it as she fought to control her ragged breathing.

What was it about that man that could disturb her so? Every word that he had said echoed again in her memory, quickening her pulse. 'I want you to be my mistress . . . I would very much like to continue where we left off . . .' A shimmer of heat ran through her. It was those eyes, so dark and mesmerising. When he looked at her in that certain way . . .

Damn, what sort of idiot was she turning into? Impatiently she shook her head, trying to dispel the images that were swirling in her brain. It was ridiculous—she should be furious at his arrogant assumption that he had only to snap his fingers and she would succumb to his practised seduction.

But she had to admit to herself that she was in serious danger of doing just that. She was almost shocked by the strength of her own reaction to him. She had never felt like that about anyone before—not David, not Craig.

Somehow the dream had got mixed up. The Wicked Baron was about to turn her grandfather out of his house. She was supposed to hate him—but she didn't. And the gallant knight who was offering to rescue her, to marry her—she wouldn't touch him with a barge-pole!

The following morning, Cassy caught the bus into Wells and went to see Grandpa's solicitor. The discussion only confirmed what Grandpa had already told her—unless they could afford to buy the freehold or a further lease, James could seek a court order for recovery of the property.

'I have made enquiries of Sir James's lawyers regarding the possibility of his accepting a statutory tenancy, but I am advised that in view of the poor state of repair to which your grandfather has allowed the property to deteriorate, they are not prepared to consider such an offer.'

'But if we had the repairs done?'

'Your grandfather had me look into that.' He picked up a thick sheaf of papers. 'I obtained estimates for the major repairs—the re-tiling of the roof, replacement of window-frames, re-wiring throughout the house, dealing with the encroachment of dry rot . . .'

Cassy held up a restraining hand. 'That sounds

expensive enough,' she commented wryly.

'It certainly is. Regrettably, Miss Durward, I have to advise you that unless you have considerable finance at your disposal, there is little you can do.'

The country bus wound its way through every village on the way home from Wells, giving Cassy plenty of time to think. She had a few thousand pounds saved up, but it would barely pay for the new roof, let alone all the other repairs that had to be done. And she wouldn't be able to get a loan, because if she stayed at home, she was going to be out of a job.

But she was going to have to stay at home. She would ring Rhoda as soon as she got in, and tell her—she would be upset, but she would have to understand that she had no choice. Grandpa needed her now—he was old and frail, he couldn't be left on his own, with only Fishy and Jenkins to look after him. They too were old now—they should both be retiring.

As she gazed out of the dusty window of the bus, she couldn't really regret the necessity of her decision. It was a beautiful spring day, bright and sunny, and the only clouds were picture-book ones of white cotton-wool. The bus crested the hill above Coombe Bradley, and shuddered its way down to the bus stop in front of the post-office. The village looked lovely—all the neatly tended front gardens were full of tulips, and the horse chestnuts on the village green were laden with white blossom. Who needed Central Park?

And here she wasn't just another face in the crowd—everyone knew her. As soon as she stepped down from the bus she was accosted by an old friend, eager to regale her with the latest piece of local gossip. 'Well, you must remember Margaret Liddle—her with the red hair, used to have the paper-shop before them Dorset people took it over. Well, it was her brother that . . .' She stopped in mid-flow as someone came out of the post office. Cassy glanced up to see James smiling down at her.

'Good afternoon, ladies. Cassy, I was hoping I'd see you,' he added. 'Can I give you a lift up the hill?'

'Oh, no, really . . .'

'It's no trouble.'

Why did his smile have the power to turn her brain to orange jelly? She knew full well that the next dozen people that Carol met would be furnished with the interesting information that Sir James was driving Cassy Durward home—and Betty in the launderette, she that's married to Sir James's chauffeur, said he took her out to dinner the other night.

James's steel-grey sports car was parked at the kerb, and Cassy's eyes ran appreciatively over its sleek, muscular lines. It was a powerful machine, as uncompromisingly masculine as its owner. Inside it was warm with the smell of leather, and she drank in its comfort as she sat back and fastened her seat-belt.

'Here,' he said as he slid into the driving-seat. 'I've got a little present for you.'

She slanted him a wary glance as he leaned over and picked up a small box from the back seat, and put it into her hands. 'What is it?' she asked suspiciously.

'Open it and see.'

She took off the lid, and unfolded the tissue paper inside. It was the little Sèvres figure. She stared up at him. 'I . . . I can't possibly accept this,' she protested.

'Why not? You were right about it, you know. I took it into Sotheby's yesterday, and they confirmed that it's a fake. Please, take it—with my thanks for saving me from the embarrassment of having my secret discovered by a less discreet expert than yourself.'

She gazed down at the figure in her hand. It was very pretty—a good copy of a work by a master. The eyes were demurely downcast, the pose natural and graceful. She would love to have it. She wrapped it up in its tissue paper again. 'Thank you,' she murmured, guiltily succumbing to temptation.

'So you're not entirely averse to taking presents from me?' he taunted softly as he gunned the powerful engine and eased the car away from the kerb.

'So long as you're not expecting anything in return,' she answered defensively.

'Such a cynical attitude! What could I possible be expecting in return?'

She slanted him an angry glance. He always seemed to twist round everything she said. 'After the things you said the other night . . .'

His smile taunted her. 'Was I too blunt for you?' he enquired mockingly. 'Would you prefer to be wooed with flowers and flattery? Should I pretend to be in love with you?'

'Of course not.'

'Quite. I'm under no illusions where you're concerned, my dear. I think it's better if we both know where we stand. So I'm making it plain right from the beginning. I want you to be my mistress, as you so quaintly put it, and I'm quite willing to pay for the pleasure. But I've no intention of marrying you.'

She slanted him a look of icy disdain. 'What makes you think I'd want to marry *you* anyway?' she enquired, her voice taut with fury.

He laughed without humour. 'Because you're a Durward, and the Durwards have always married money,' he answered bluntly.

She blinked at him in astonishment. 'That's not true!' she protested indignantly.

'No?' His voice was a whiplash of contempt. 'What about your father—the Honorable William Anthony St John Durward? He traded on his title for years, until he found an impressionable young heiress to marry. It didn't take him long to run through her fortune, did it? They were living on fresh air by the time they were killed.'

Cassy flushed, remembering all those horrible stories in the newspapers when she was young. She had dismissed them all as cheap lies.

'And then of course there was your grand-father,' James went on, a bitter edge of sarcasm in his voice. 'He'd gambled away practically every penny he had by the time he was twenty-five, and then he thought he's set himself up again by marrying my great-aunt Elizabeth.'

Her eyes flashed. 'He didn't! He adored her,' she insisted forcefully. 'He's always talking about her.'

'She adored him—she wouldn't hear a word against him. She pestered my great-grandfather until he gave in, and let her marry him. But he even took her to Monte Carlo for their honeymoon, and spent all his time in the casino, and lost every penny of the allowance my great-grandfather had given her for the whole year. In the end, she had to admit that my great-grandfather had been right, and it broke her heart.'

'You're lying,' she protested weakly.

'Why should I lie?' he asked reasonably. 'If you don't believe me, ask your Mrs Fisher. She was devoted to her—the only reason she stayed with your grandfather was that she promised her she would.' He drew up outside Grandpa's house, and she began fumbling to release her seat-belt. But before she could open the door and escape, he had come round to open it for her. 'When am I going to see you again?' he asked, resting his hand against the car so that she was effectively trapped.

She met his eyes defiantly. 'You're not,' she snapped.

'You won't have dinner with me tomorrow night?'

'No, thank you.'

'Oh dear. Giving up the game already? Are you so afraid of defeat?'

She tilted her chin at a proud angle. 'Not at all,'

she returned coldly. 'There isn't the least risk of that.'

'No? Well, let's wait and see, shall we?'

Her anger was threating to explode inside her skull. She took a deep, steadying breath. 'Sir James, let me make it plain that I have no wish for any kind of relationship with you. Now will you please let me go?'

'Haven't you forgotten something?' She stared at him blankly. 'I gave you a present.'

'Thank you,' she retorted haughtily. 'But I've changed my mind about accepting it. Good afternoon, Sir James.'

He smiled with mocking satisfaction. 'Good afternoon, Miss Durward,' he taunted, standing aside to let her pass.

She almost ran up the garden path, cursing herself for letting him get to her like that as she fumbled in her bag for her key. She let herself in, and ran straight on up the stairs to her own room, where she threw herself down on the bed, and buried her face in the pillow.

His words were spinning in her head. He was lying—he *must* have been lying. And yet . . . suddenly a few things had started to make sense to her—things she shouldn't have overheard when she was a child, things people had started to say and then stopped themselves. She had begun to realise a long time ago that Grandpa's gambling went further than just the occasional gentlemanly flutter on the horses—it was far more serious than that. When Grandpa came home, she would talk to him. It really was time she knew the truth. He ought to be home in time for lunch.

But it was late afternoon when the car finally drew up outside the house, and as she hurried down the path to greet him, she saw that Michael Farrell was with him. Her footsteps hesitated, but in the next instant she realised that something was wrong.

'Grandpa? What's the matter? Are you ill?' she asked as she pulled open the car door.

'Ah, Miss Durward,' Michael greeted her with a grave smile. 'I'm afraid he's been feeling poorly since this morning.'

She glanced at him coldly. 'Then why didn't you telephone me, or at least get a doctor to him, instead of letting him drive all this way?' she demanded angrily.

'He absolutely insisted . . .'

Cassy ignored him as she helped Grandpa carefully out of the car and up the path to the house. He leaned heavily on her arm as if feeling every one of his seventy-nine years. She took him into his sitting-room, and he slumped into his favourite armchair.

'Can I get you anything?' she asked solicitously.

'Just . . . just a little brandy.'

She hurried to pour him a drink of his favourite cognac from the cut-glass decanter on the sideboard. Michael had followed them into the room uninvited, and casually helped himself to a generous three fingers of the brandy. She slanted him a glance of icy disdain.

'I'm sorry, indeed, Miss Durward,' he murmured apologetically. 'I did try to persuade him not to undertake the journey.'

'You could have telephoned me.'

'He wouldn't hear of it.'

She pulled a wry face. 'He can be rather obstinate at times,' she conceded.

'I'm afraid so. What will you do? Will you call a doctor?'

She glanced over her shoulder at Grandpa. He was leaning back in his chair, his eyes closed. She frowned. Sometimes Grandpa could be a little inclined to over-dramatise his health when it suited him. But she didn't want to take any risks.

'Yes, I think I should.' She went over to him, and touched his arm gently. 'Grandpa?' He opened his eyes again, and smiled at her bravely. 'I'm going to call Dr Marshall,' she told him.

He nodded, reaching for the glass of brandy she was holding. 'You do whatever you think fit,' he conceded in a feeble voice.

She bit her lip. She had been arguing with him all week about seeing the doctor, but he had adamantly refused. His capitulation worried her even more than his sagging shoulders. She hurried out to the hall, and picked up the telephone.

Dr Marshall's verdict did little to resolve her anxiety. 'Well, he's remarkably fit for his age,' he told her. 'But he is nearly eighty, and he ought to be taking it easy. You should make him give up those cigars, you know.'

Cassy laughed wryly. 'You're joking.'

He smiled. 'Well, yes. He is a stubborn old goat. But it would certainly do him good to take a bit more care of himself. When are you planning to return to New York?'

'I'm not,' she told him. 'I did only come over for a holiday, but I've decided to stay—Grandpa needs me.'

The doctor nodded. 'Good, good. Not that I think it's anything serious this time, but you can never be too careful. I'll pop in tomorrow and see how he's getting along.'

'Fine. Thank you very much for coming, Doctor. Goodbye.'

Michael had made himself at home on the settee in Grandpa's sitting-room, sitting back with his legs crossed, his brandy-glass refreshed for the second time since his arrival. 'What did the doctor have to say, then?' he asked.

'Simply that he should rest,' she responded. 'Grandpa, do you think you can climb the stairs now? You ought to lie down for a little while.'

'No, no. Leave me alone, let me sit here,' he grumbled impatiently. 'I'm comfortable here. How about another brandy?'

'I don't really think you should.'

'Is that what that old quack said?' he demanded irascibly. 'He doesn't know what he's talking about. It's medicinal, brandy, everyone knows that. Come on, be a good girl.' He held out his empty glass peremptorily.

Michael showed no inclination to leave, and eventually she was forced to invite him to dinner. It was all she could do to be pleasant to him during the meal; though she couldn't really complain of his manners, she didn't care much for his sense of humour, nor the way he tended to let his gaze rest on her body every time he spoke to her, instead of meeting her eyes.

After dinner she contrived to escape, making the excuse of helping Fishy in the kitchen. She was still curious about the things that James had said. She glanced at Fishy as she took a wet plate from her and carefully dried it and placed it on the stack on the table. What fifty-year-old secrets lay behind that placid face?

'How old were you when you first came to work for Grandpa?' she asked curiously.

'Oh, I'd have been about fourteen,' Fishy told her. 'My Aunt Emily was cook up at the Big House.'

'Yes, I know. Didn't you ever want to do something different?'

'Oh, no. Well, what would I want to do? Go and work in some factory? Not me. And of course I had my eye on my Harry—Lord Bradley's chauffeur, he was then. Not that I'd have been allowed to walk out with him—we was very strictly kept in those days.'

'Was that before Grandpa was married?' Cassy persisted carefully.

Fishy nodded. 'Yes, though Miss Elizabeth was here all the time, Lord Bradley and Sir Giles were great friends at that time. Of course, that was before . . .'

'Before what?'

A guarded look came across the housekeeper's broad face. 'I thought you was down here to help me with the washing up?' she challenged. 'I don't have time for all this gabbling.'

Cassy laughed. 'We can talk and work at the same time. Wasn't Sir Giles pleased when his sister married his best friend?'

'Not exactly,' conceded Fishy carefully.

'Why not?'

Fishy heaved a heavy sigh. 'Don't be asking me these things, Miss Cassy,' she pleaded. 'I've kept my peace all these years . . .'

Cassy put down the tea-towel, and went over to hug the good woman's plump arm. 'Don't get upset, Fishy,' she pleaded. 'But don't you think I'm old enough now to know the truth?'

'It's your Grandpa you should be asking . . .'

'Grandpa lives in a dream,' Cassy told her insistently. 'I don't think he even remembers any more what the truth really is.'

Fishy nodded sadly, and moved over to sit down heavily in the battered old rocking-chair in front of what had once been a working range. 'Ah, that's the way of it,' she agreed, drying her hands on her apron. 'Very well, then, I'll tell you.'

Cassy sat on the floor, and waited for her to begin.

'He was a wilful boy, was Lord Bradley. He never had his father's hand to guide him, and his mother was a weak, doting woman. He'd run himself into debt with the money-lenders before he even came of age. Once he had his hands on his fortune, there was no holding him—it ran through his hands like water.

'Old Mr Clayton, Sir Giles's father, tried to take him under his wing, for his father's sake, but it did no good. All it did was give Miss Elizabeth the chance to lose her heart to him. Ah, she was a lovely girl—and laugh! She was like a song-bird.' She wiped away a tear with the corner of her apron.

'That was when her father tried to put his foot down. But it was already too late—nothing would do for her but to marry her darling Edwin, no matter how they warned her. And you never saw such a happy bride—even the sun was dimmed by comparison. But little by little he broke her heart, until she couldn't take no more.

'I'm not saying it was right what she done—I was always taught in church that it was a sin. But she left me a note—I'd come down to be her maid when they moved from the Big House—and a locket. I didn't find them till after she'd gone out, and none of us knew where she'd gone. Lord Bradley was away at the races,' she added bitterly. 'He didn't know nothing about it till it was all over, and all he had to do was cry crocodile tears over her grave.'

She leaned over, and opened a drawer, and took out a small silver locket which she put into Cassy's hand. 'This is the only picture there is of her,' she said. 'Lord Bradley had them all taken down—he'd come to regret what he'd done, when it was too late to put right.'

Cassy gazed at the tiny picture in the locket. A lovely face was laughing up at her—younger than she was now, full of innocence and vulnerability. 'Oh,' she murmured, 'wasn't she beautiful!'

'That she was,' agreed Fishy, taking the locket

back and looking at the picture with a smile of sad reminiscence. 'Sometimes it seems like it was only yesterday.' She put the locket away, and shut the drawer. 'Well, this isn't getting the chores done,' she grumbled briskly. 'Go on with you, off upstairs now so I can get finished up.'

Cassy didn't argue. She walked slowly up the stairs, deep in thought. It seemed as if the whole world had been turned upside down, all her perceptions were going to have to be re-assembled. Grandpa's stories about the way he had been cheated were all lies—and the stories about her parents were true. So what did that make her? She had always held herself with a certain pride, sure that although her family had little money at least they had honour. Now that confidence was gone.

As she reached the dimly-lit hall, a shadow fell across her path, and she looked up, startled, to see Michael Farrell above her. 'Ah, there you are, my pretty,' he purred, his grey eyes sliding over her with that smug insolence that made her flesh crawl.

Her fingers curled tightly around the banister rail. 'So it would appear,' she returned tartly.

He chuckled. 'Ah, ye've a sharp tongue in your head, all right. But you'd do well to learn not to use it on me.'

'Oh?' She let her lip curl into a sneer. 'Well, if you don't like my manners, you know what you can do, don't you?'

She tried to brush past him, but he blocked her way with his arm, and she found herself cornered against the wall. 'You know, I think it's time you and I had a little talk,' he said.

'I don't think we've anything to talk about.'

'Ah, but we have. There's a little matter of the lease on this house. Not to mention the money the old man owes me.'

She stared at him, aghast. 'My grandfather owes you money? I don't believe it!'

'Why don't you ask him?' he taunted.

Her confidence wavered in the face of his certainty, but she lifted her chin at a proud angle. 'How much does he owe you?' she enquired coolly.

'Forty thousand pounds.'

'What?' She felt faint. 'How . . . how could he have possibly borrowed that sort of money from you?'

His smile was mocking. 'Well, your Grandpa has this little weakness, you see. And I was happy to indulge him. I'm afraid the horses just weren't running for him. If you had been a little more amenable to my plans . . .'

'You think you can make me agree to marry you?'

He let his eyes linger greedily over every curve of her body. 'Oh yes, I think so. You wouldn't want to see the poor old man in the bankruptcy court, now would you?'

Her eyes flashed in cold fury, and she tried to push past him, but he had his hand on her waist, pinning her against the wall. 'If Grandpa knew what you were scheming . . .' she hissed.

He laughed maliciously. 'Ah, but you're not going to tell him, are you?' he taunted. 'Why upset him, to no purpose? After all, where else would you get all that money, eh?'

She shivered in horror. Forty thousand pounds! It was almost unbelievable—and yet after what she had just learned . . .

'So, my pretty,' he went on smugly, 'you don't really have any choice, do you? Oh, I know you think you're too good for me, but I'm going to enjoy teaching you a bit of respect. You're a fine-looking woman.' His eyes leered down into hers, and he let his hand slide slowly up to squeeze her breast. 'Mmm—nice.'

She froze in revulsion, but forced herself to meet his gaze levelly. 'You make me feel sick,' she enunciated in a voice that would strip paint.

He laughed, but he let her go, and she shoved past him. Grandpa was in his sitting-room, and he looked up as she burst into the room, a comfortable smile on his face.

'Ah there you are, my dear. What a good girl you are, helping Fishy like that, when I know who you'd have rather been with.'

She closed the door, and leaned against it, her breathing ragged as she fought to control the churning emotions inside her. How could she be angry with poor Grandpa? Whatever his failings, he was a dear, frail old man. When she was a little girl, and had wanted a kitten, it was Grandpa who had brought one home for her, hidden in a cardboard box. And when she and her pony had been winning all the rosettes in the county it had been Grandpa who had stood on the side-lines, applauding proudly.

She forced herself to smile. 'I like helping Fishy,' she insisted with an assumption of cheerfulness.

He chuckled archly. 'Ah, I know what it is. You're playing hard to get,' he teased her. 'Well, I'll let you into a little secret. You've scored a very big hit indeed.' He smiled down at her proudly. 'Now what do you think of that?'

She made herself pretend innocent enquiry. 'What do you mean, Granpda?' she asked.

'Why, Michael of course. Now, I know I might be jumping the gun a little, but I just want you to know that nothing would make me happier.'

Her breath escaped in a silent sigh. Michael was right—she couldn't bring herself to disillusion him. Somehow she was going to have to find a way out of this disaster by herself. But how? Forty thousand pounds . . . It might as well be a million!

Behind her the door opened, and Michael himself came into the room. His eyes glittered as he glanced at her, but he was all phony charm as he turned to Grandpa. 'Well, Edwin, I'll be saying goodbye then. I'll ring tomorrow to see that you're well.'

'Oh, I'm fine, I'm fine,' Grandpa declared expansively. 'But are you sure you have to be going? You'd be more than welcome to stay for a while, wouldn't he, Cassy?'

'I'm sure Michael knows exactly how welcome he is in this house,' she murmured with deceptive sweetness.

'Ah, 'tis very kind of you, Cassy, to be sure,' he returned, smiling like a snake. 'But I'm afraid I really do have to be going—I've stables to run, after all. But I'll be seeing you again very soon.' The expression in his eyes indicated that she could take that as a warning.

'Well, goodbye then, Michael,' conceded Granpda, offering the younger man his hand. 'Cassy will see you to the door.'

'Goodbye, Edwin. Take care of yourself, now.' The two men shook hands in warm farewell, and then Michael followed Cassy out into the hall. 'You see?' he murmured mockingly. 'The old man thinks I'm the ideal grandson-in-law.'

'Then he's in for a disappointment,' she countered tartly.

'Ah now, you shouldn't be so hasty,' he advised, his voice quiet with menace. 'Not unless you can get your hands on a great deal of money at short notice.'

'H . . . how short?' she demanded unsteadily.

'Shall we say tomorrow night?' he purred. 'I've a mind to take you out to dinner. To celebrate our engagement.'

She hesitated, her throat constricting. She would have loved to be able to tell him exactly where to go, but she couldn't. She was trapped. 'Very well,' she managed to say. 'I . . . I'll give you my decision tomorrow night.'

CHAPTER SIX

IT WAS late when Cassy at last fell into a troubled sleep, and when she woke her nightmares were still with her. Where on earth was she going to get forty thousand pounds—as well as the money to purchase the lease on the house? For a brief moment she entertained the idea of asking Rhoda, or even Craig, but she couldn't do that—how would she ever pay them back?

There was only one other person she knew with that sort of money—and he did want something from her. A shimmer of heat ran through her. James wanted her to be his mistress. She lay back on the pillows, and closed her eyes. Yesterday morning she had had no hesitation in rejecting his suggestion with contempt, but now . . .

Yesterday morning, she had believed that he was the scion of a house of scoundrels, tainted with their guilt himself. But now she knew that his family had been the innocent parties, and her own the villains of the tale. Somehow that seemed to alter the whole framework of their relationship—as if a see-saw had swung him up into the air, and her down to the ground.

If it weren't for the money, would she be his mistress? An uncomfortably honest corner of her mind had to confess that the temptation was almost too strong to resist. Oh, she knew he wasn't actually in love with her, but he was certainly strongly attracted to her. Could that be enough?

She had always believed that only a deep commitment of the heart could lead her into such a relationship, had somehow assumed that marriage would enter into it somewhere. But the attraction she felt towards James was beyond all her experience, it didn't fit into any of her preconceived ideas. It made its own rules.

Yes—if it wasn't for the money, she could easily cast her fate to the winds, ignore the inevitable gossip, lose herself in the intoxicating pleasures that she had glimpsed all too briefly when he had kissed her. But the money was not something that she could set aside. And how could she ask him for forty thousand pounds, in the same breath as she promised to be his mistress? She might as well walk the streets of Times Square.

And so the only alternative left was to marry Michael Farrell. A wave of nausea swept over her as she remembered the way he had looked at her, the way he had touched her. She was going to have to submit to those greedy hands, as the price of saving Grandpa from his own folly, and letting him spend the last years of his life in peace and dignity.

As if in sympathy with her mood, it rained all day, a steady dull drizzle. Cassy spent most of the day in her room, curled up on the window-seat, staring out dismally at the garden, trying in vain to think of some other way out of her predicament. But by evening she was forced to admit that she had no choice but to reconcile herself to her fate. Her heart was heavy as she began to get ready for her dinner-date.

The black dress was back from the cleaners, fully restored, and she coiled her hair into an upswept, touch-me-not style. Then she stood staring at her own reflection in the mirror. 'Why don't you think of something?' she demanded of the immaculately groomed image. 'This is the twentieth century, for goodness' sake. This kind of thing doesn't happen any more.' But the cool blonde in the mirror could think of no reply, and with a sigh she went downstairs.

Michael was lounging on the settee in Grandpa's sitting-room, a large tumbler of Grandpa's expensive whisky in his hand. He let his eyes linger over her in undisguised approval. 'My, don't you look beautiful?' he purred with satisfaction.

She returned him a frosty glare. 'Shall we go?' she asked.

'Of course, of course. I'll say goodnight then, Edwin. You'll be abed when I bring your girl home, no doubt.'

Grandpa smiled contentedly. 'Oh, yes—off you go, and have a good time,' he urged them innocently.

Cassy bent and kissed him on the cheek. 'Goodnight, Grandpa,' she murmured, hiding her pain. 'I'll see you in the morning.' Then she turned to Michael, and let him draw her hand through his arm, and lead her out to his car.

'I'm glad you chose to see sense,' remarked Michael as they walked down the garden path. 'It would have been a pity to cause him any distress.'

'Yes,' she agreed tersely, eyeing his car with misgiving. It was a foreign-built turbo-charged sports car, not designed with the comfort of its passengers in mind. 'I don't know if I'm going to have enough head-room in this,' she murmured dubiously.

'Ah, now, 'tis a little low-slung, to be sure, but you'll be very comfortable once you're inside.' He opened the door for her, and she slid into the passenger seat. 'Nice little motor, isn't she?' he remarked as he started the engine. 'She's got more than two hundred brake horse-power at four thousand rpm. The engine displaces a little under three thousand cc, and she's got a top speed of nearly one-forty and nought-to-sixty in just over seven seconds.'

Instinctively Cassy gripped the sides of her seat as he accelerated sharply, speeding down the hill and swerving across the bridge. 'Thank you, there's no need to demonstrate,' she assured him drily.

He chuckled with laughter. 'Ah, now, you needn't worry,' he assured her. 'I'm a very good driver. We're going to a rather a nice little place I know, down by the river. It's rather exclusive—you usually have to book in advance, but I'm on excellent terms with the *maître d'*, so we'll have no trouble getting a table.'

Fortunately his conversation required little response from her. She sat back in her seat, watching the scenery roll by. The route was familiar, and it was no surprise when they drew up before the black and white inn on the river.

'Here we are. You'll like it here,' Michael announced smugly as he came round to open the car door for her.

'I've been before,' she informed him with satisfaction as she swept regally past him.

The liveried doorman recognised her, and smiled as he bowed them into the hall. But the head waiter was not hovering inside, as he had on her previous visit. Instead, Michael had to accost a junior waiter as he hurried across the hall with a bundle of menus.

'*Pardon, m'sieur.* I will return in one moment,' he responded politely.

Cassy fixed her attention on the intricate linen-fold

panelling, studiously ignoring Michael as he paced impatiently about the hall. The waiter swiftly returned. 'My apologies, *m'sieur. M'sieur* has reserved a table?'

'No, as a matter of fact I haven't.' Michael took out his bulging wallet, and flicked it open, but the waiter shook his head apologetically. 'I regret, *m'sieur,* we are very busy tonight.'

Michael extracted a ten-pound note and crinkled it under the waiter's unimpressed gaze. 'Well then, where's the *maître d'?'* he demanded.

At that moment Claude himself materialised. 'Is there some difficulty?' he enquired smoothly.

'None at all, if I can have a table.'

'I regret . . .' But as Cassy turned towards them, his expression was transformed. 'Ah, *mademoiselle!* But of course—I am happy to welcome you again to the Mermaid. I am sure we can find you a table. Please, come with me.'

Cassy allowed herself a flicker of amusement at the chagrin on Michael's face as she followed Claude into the restaurant. It was not crowded, and the first person she saw was James. Her heart skidded and lurched into a higher gear.

He was at a table with two other men and three women. She couldn't tear her eyes away. One of the women was older, but the other two were young, and undeniably beautiful, and from the way he was sharing his attention equally between the two of them she couldn't tell which one he was with.

He glanced up, and saw her across the room, and that slow smile curved his cynical mouth. With a supreme effort of will, Cassy moved forward again, following Claude. As she came up to James's table, he rose to his feet, impeccably polite.

'Good evening, Miss Durward. What a pleasant surprise.' The mockery in his voice was so refined as to be barely discernible.

She tilted her chin at a proud angle. 'Good evening, Sir James,' she responded coolly. His dark eyes flickered towards Michael, and she saw in them a hint of cool distaste. 'May I introduce . . .'

'Ah, indeed, but there's no need to introduce us,' interrupted Michael, offering his hand. 'We've met before, Sir James.'

James ignored the proffered hand. 'So I believe,' he responded distantly.

Cassy felt her cheeks flush a heated red—there was no mistaking his contempt. She took Michael's arm urgently. 'Come on, our table's ready,' she reminded him, drawing him away.

They followed Claude to a good but less exclusive part of the restaurant. She chose to sit with her back to James, but discovered almost at once that she could see his reflection in a large gilded mirror on the opposite wall. The waiter brought the menu, and she made her selection absent-mindedly, aware of those dark eyes watching her in the glass.

'Do you prefer red or white?' She glanced up in blank enquiry. 'Which wine?' Michael repeated.

'Oh . . .' She had already forgotten what she had ordered to eat. 'You choose.'

He nodded, pleased by her deference, but she was paying him little attention. She was covertly watching James in the mirror, noting every smile he bestowed on the two girls at his table. They seemed to be equally charmed by him, and Cassy felt a stab of annoyance. No wonder he had such a fine opinion of himself, if silly girls like that could only simper and make cow-eyes at him.

She looked away again quickly as his dark gaze met hers in the glass. She barely noticed what she was eating, and her only comment on the wine would have been that it was a little too brash. Michael seemed to be enjoying it, though, and ordered a second bottle. Added to the whisky he had already drunk with Grandpa while waiting for her, it was beginning to colour his countenance.

He seemed oblivious of her distraction, whiling away the meal with repetitive anecdotes of his racing career, droping names like confetti. She listened with half an ear, occasionally interjecting a suitable comment, glad to be spared the chore of conversing with him. Suddenly he scowled across the room.

'That chap Clayton—is he something to you?'

She glanced up at him in surprise. 'Of course not,' she answered quickly.

'Then why does he keep looking at you?'

'I've really no idea,' she said, her hand shaking as she stirred a little sugar into her coffee.

'You'd best be telling me the truth, me darling,' he warned her. 'I wouldn't want to find that you were playing around behind my back.' He scowled as he picked up the wine bottle and found it empty. 'Hey, waiter,' he called a little louder than was necessary. 'Let's have a large brandy here.'

Cassy regarded him coldly across the table. 'Don't forget you're driving home,' she reminded him. 'Don't you think you're over the limit?'

'Ah now, darlin', don't be nagging me,' he grumbled. 'We're not married yet.'

'No—and I'm not sure that we're going to be,' she returned, too angry to guard her tongue.

He chuckled with laughter. 'Ah, you've plenty of spirit, right enough,' he taunted. 'But I like that. A beautiful woman is like a racehorse—all the better for a bit of spirit.'

'Indeed?'

He smiled, impervious to the frosty note in her voice. 'D'ye know, I think we'll get on famously together,' he declared expansively.

'I take leave to doubt that,' she returned. 'Now I would like to go home.'

'Ah now, Cassy, me darlin' . . .'

'My name is Cassandra,' she snapped. 'And I am *not* your darling.' She rose to her feet, and with a tolerable assumption of composure walked out of the restaurant, refusing to let her eyes be drawn by James as she passed his table.

Claude hurried forward anxiously. 'Was the meal satisfactory, *mademoiselle?*'

'Perfectly, thank you,' she responded with dignity. 'Could you please call a taxi for me?'

Michael caught up with her in the hall, and snatched at her arm. 'You stuck-up bitch,' he snarled, his face ugly with anger. 'It's a lesson you need.'

'Possibly,' intervened a sardonic voice behind them. 'But I don't think you're the one to give it to her.' Cassy glanced up in astonishment as James coolly took her arm. 'May I give you a lift home, Miss Durward?'

'Hey, who the hell do you think you are?' protested Michael furiously. 'The lady's with me.'

'She *was* with you. She appears to have had second thoughts,' James countered, a hint of warning in his voice.

But Michael was in no mood to be so casually dismissed. 'You don't just walk out on me, Miss High-and-Mighty Durward,' he snarled, grabbing her other arm in a painful grasp.

'Let me go!' she protested, trying to struggle free.

He raised his hand to strike her, and she flinched away, and the next moment he was sprawled on the ground, a trickle of blood on his lip. She stared down at him, appalled. She had provoked this situation herself, by her reluctance to submit to the inevitable, and now alarming visions of the consequences rose before her.

'Michael!' she cried anxiously, dropping to her knees beside him.

'Leave him,' rapped James harshly. 'He hasn't broken anything—I didn't hit him hard enough.' He took her arm again, and dragged her to her feet. 'Come on, I'll take you home.'

'No!' She tried to shake him off, but his grip tightened. 'You don't understand.'

'Oh, I think I understand all too well,' he sneered, hustling her through the front doors. 'But you can do a lot better for yourself than that, you know.' The Aston Martin was parked outside, and he opened the passenger door for her. 'Get in,' he commanded imperiously.

She turned to face him, breathless and defiant. 'What about your dinner companions?' she enquired, instilling a sharp edge of sarcasm into her voice. 'Won't they think it's odd of you to just disappear like this?'

'I'm more than grateful to you for giving me an excuse to escape,' he told her, an inflection of sardonic humour in his voice. 'I'm afraid the atmosphere was becoming a little . . . competitive.'

'Over you, I suppose?' she returned, her eyes flashing. 'You really are the most arrogant . . .'

'You've told me that before,' he countered infuriatingly. 'Now get in the car.' He leaned towards her, as if threatening to kiss her, and the only place she could retreat was into the car. He closed the door on her, and came round quickly to the driver's seat. As he gunned the engine she leaned back in her seat, closing her eyes, trembling with reaction.

'You'd better put your seat-belt on.'

She fumbled to obey. The car swept out of the car park and on to the open road, gathering speed.

'I can't say I think much of your taste,' remarked James, cold contempt in his voice. 'I've heard Farrell's got plenty of money, but I've never noticed that he's particularly over-burdened with charm.'

'No,' she agreed wryly.

'So why were you dining with him?'

'It's a long story.'

'No doubt.'

'And I don't see that it's particularly any of your business,' she added defensively.

'Probably not. I didn't realise that that was the sort of treatment you liked. Perhaps I should try being a little bit rough with you myself.'

'I don't like it,' she returned tensely.

'You certainly seemed to be showing a great deal of concern for his health.'

'You didn't have to hit him like that.'

'Oh, I'm sorry,' he drawled with biting sarcasm. 'I'm afraid it was an instinctive reaction. I've this peculiar aversion to seeing a man hitting a woman.'

Cassy fell silent. What could she say? After that scene in the restaurant, she *couldn't* marry Michael— even if he still wanted her. It was one thing to force herself to accept his sickening sexual advances, it was something else entirely to submit to his violence.

And so now there really was only one thing left. Her fists clenched tightly in her lap. What if she

asked him, and he refused? Forty thousand pounds
—it was an awful lot of money. And worse, it was
going to convince him that he had been right about
her all along—that she really was the sort of woman
who was for sale, if the price was right. It would be a
waste of time to try to explain why she needed it—it
would sound like a very pathetic excuse.

Tears stung the backs of her eyes as she gazed
bleakly out of the window. There was no moon, and
the stars looked cold and remote against the
blackness of the sky. But the car was a warm cocoon
of luxury, pale grey leather and gleaming burr-
walnut. It was as if they were in a capsule, hurtling
through space, the only two people in all the vast
infinity of the night.

James had turned on the in-car stereo, and the
low, haunting music of a tenor saxophone drifted
around them like coils of blue smoke. She found herself watching his hands on the steering-wheel, effortlessly controlling the powerful car. They were strong
hands, but well made, with long, sensitive fingers.
Beneath his crisp white shirt cuffs his thick wrists
showed a smattering of fine dark hair, and the
discreet gold gleam of a Rolex watch.

Slowly she let her eyes wander up past the broad
cliff of his shoulder to study the hard lines of his
face. In the fleeting bright gleam of the headlights of
approaching cars it was a hunter's face, ruthless and
intelligent. An odd little chill scudded along her spine.

'Are you cold?'

She lowered her lashes in swift defensiveness as the
dark gleam of his eyes turned towards her. 'No,' she
managed to answer, her voice constricted. In the con-
fined space of the car that raw masculinity created a
tension that was almost unbearable.

He laughed softly. 'If I didn't know you better I might think you were nervous,' he taunted. 'But of course, you don't even like me. And you've *certainly* no intention of letting me seduce you.' He slanted her a glance of mocking enquiry. 'Have you?'

Cassy had to swallow the constriction in her throat. It was now or never. 'You . . . you said you'd be prepared to pay for the pleasure,' she heard herself say.

'So I did,' returned James, a question in his voice.

'H . . . how much?'

The temperature in the car seemed suddenly several degrees lower, and James's voice was a whiplash of contempt. 'How much do you want?'

She was clenching her fists so tightly in her lap that her fingers hurt. 'You . . . you hold the lease on my grandfather's house,' she began with difficulty.

'So I believe,' he conceded, a question in his voice.

'And it's due to expire in a few weeks.'

'Is it? I'll have to take your word for it. All my property affairs are dealt with by my legal department. They don't trouble me with every detail.'

'It may be a detail to you,' she retorted tensely, 'but it's rather important to me. That's Grandpa's home—it'll break his heart to leave it.'

'So?'

'So . . . I want you to let him stay—as a proper tenant, paying rent.'

A flicker of a smile crossed his hard mouth. 'Is that all?' he enquired cordially.

She drew a deep breath. She had to say it. 'And I want forty thousand pounds.'

He whistled through his teeth. 'You do place a high value on yourself,' he remarked drily.

'Do you want me to be your mistress or not?' she

demanded, the pain of humiliation lending a rough edge to her voice.

'At that price, I might need a little persuading.'

They were almost home, but abruptly he spun the car off the road, and into the shadow of the trees. 'W . . . where are we going?' she stammered.

'For a walk,' he answered roughly. 'Come on.'

He got out of the car, and set off at a brisk pace. She hesitated for a moment, and then followed him. His anger was plainly written in the line of his shoulders—but it was his own fault, she thought bitterly. He was the one who had brought up the subject of money in the first place.

The path led up through the trees, to a place that in summer was a popular picnic spot, overlooking the whole valley. A couple of rustic benches had been put there by the council, and James sat on one, stretching his long legs out in front of him. Cassy stood a little distance away, watching him uncertainly. It was cold, and she rubbed her hands over her arms to warm the goose-bumps.

'You're not making a very good job of persuading me,' he taunted, without looking at her.

'I . . . I'm sorry. I don't have much experience of this sort of thing,' she mumbled.

'Oh, of course, I forgot,' he sneered scornfully. 'You're claiming to be a virgin, aren't you?' He held out an imperious hand. 'Come here.' She walked towards him, her heart pounding so fast that she felt weak. He took her hand, and pulled her down beside him. 'Do I get a refund if I find out you're lying?'

'I—I'm not lying,' she stammered.

'No?' He laced his fingers into her hair, and drew her close. 'Well, it won't be long before I find out, will it?'

His cruel mouth descended on hers, crushing her lips in a kiss that was pure punishment. She dared offer no resistance as his tongue swept deep into the sweet, defenceless valley of her mouth, plundering every corner. He had loosed the grips from her hair, and as it cascaded down he twisted his hand deliberately into its strands, holding her head back so that her body was curved helplessly across his lap.

But she was immune to the cold and discomfort. Her whole body was aflame beneath his touch as he caressed her from shoulder to thigh, insolently asserting his right to enjoy every intimacy. Fleetingly the thought passed through her mind that she ought to be offering some objection, or at least that she shouldn't be luxuriating in her martyrdom like this. But she couldn't help herself.

She felt him slide the thin strap of her dress down over her shoulder, and brush the fabric away from the aching swell of her breast. He lifted his head briefly to gaze down at the ripe curve, naked in the pale light of the stars, the rosy peak puckering beneath the teasing touch of his fingers.

'Beautiful . . .'

A shudder of pure pleasure ran through her, and she gasped on a sobbing breath as he lifted her in his arms, and his jaw rasped over her silken skin as his scorching kisses trailed down the slender column of her throat. Her head tipped dizzily back as his sensous tongue swirled around the sensitive bud of her nipple, and then his hot mouth closed over it and began to suckle, pulsing white fire through her viens.

His hand dropped to lift the hem of her skirt, and began to stroke slowly up over her silk-clad thighs. She quivered at the unfamiliar intimacy of that touch, but she could do nothing to stop him. If he had wanted to make love to her right then she would have had to let him, but at last he lifted his head again.

'I don't think this is quite the place to continue this,' he murmured smokily. 'I've a large and very comfortable bed at home . . .'

She shook her head in instinctive denial. 'No.'

'No?' A look of cold anger crossed his face. He pushed her away from him and stood up. 'Of course,' he sneered in icy cynicism. 'You want your money first.' He thrust his hands deep into his pockets as he walked away from her to stand looking down into the wide valley. 'Forty thousand, I think you said?'

She couldn't even look at him. She hung her head so that her hair veiled her face, and her voice was barely a whisper. 'Yes.'

He turned back to her. She fumbled clumsily to straighten her dress, blinking back the tears of humiliation that were stinging her eyes. 'Very well,' he said coldly. 'You'll get it. But I'm not prepared to agree to the rest of your terms.' She looked up at him in alarm. 'Once I accept rent from your grandfather, he's got a protected tenancy—I won't be able to throw him out. Then what's to stop you cheating on our deal, and scuttling back to New York with the cash?'

'I . . . I wouldn't do that,' she promised desperately.

He laughed softly. 'Oh, those eyes! But I'm not going to trust you one inch, my dear. Your grandfather can stay in the house on sufferance—rent-free. I won't take any steps to evict him, so long as you continue to please me.'

'And . . . and if I don't please you?' she managed

to ask.

His smile held a hint of warning. 'You'd better see that you do, hadn't you?' he warned. 'As soon as my cheque is cleared into your bank account, you can move in with me.'

'But . . . I can't . . . I mean, everyone will know . . .'

He laughed, and drew her into his arms, overcoming her feeble protests. 'Of course they will. I'm paying you a great deal of money—part of the pleasure of ownership is having everyone envy you.'

'Ownership?' She tried to twist away from him. 'Is that what you call it?'

'What else? And you'd better remember it, my dear.' His hands slid slowly down the length of her spine to mould her intimately against him. 'You're mine for as long as I want you. I'll pay you a decent allowance, so you'll have nothing to do but look beautiful—you should find that easy.'

'And what happens when you've had enough of me?' she enquired tautly.

He shrugged his wide shoulders in cool indifference. 'You can do what you like—find yourself a rich husband if you want. What I'll teach you should more than make up for what I'll be taking from you.'

'And Grandpa?'

He laughed mockingly. 'Oh, I might even give you a new lease on the house—as severance pay.'

That pain of humiliation twisted like a knife in her heart. 'You make it sound like . . .'

'Like what . . .'

She buried her face in the hollow of his shoulder. 'You know what I mean,' she whispered.

He laughed softly. 'Do you know, I don't think

you're really cut out for this sort of thing, my dear,' he murmured. He twisted his hand into her hair again, pulling her head back and making her look up at him. 'Admit it—if I hadn't let you go, I could have had you for nothing, couldn't I?'

'N . . . no,' she protested weakly.

'Oh yes I could. You're lucky that I want more than just a one-night stand from you, Cassy. I want you in my bed, every night. I want to be able to reach out in the night and feel your body beside me—warm, and soft, and willing.'

His mouth closed over hers again, this time gentle and enticing, his tongue swirling languorously over the delicate inner membranes of her lips, re-lighting the fires inside her. She clung to him as if she were falling, her mind a cauldron of emotions. She *couldn't* be falling in love with him. It wasn't possible. He was arrogant, and cynical, and he had made it plain that he wanted only one thing from her.

She drew back out of his arms. 'C—can we go home now?' she pleaded, avoiding his eyes. 'It's cold up here.'

'If you like,' he agreed, an inflection of ironic humour in his voice. 'Here, you'd better put this on—I don't want you freezing to death.' He took off his jacket, and wrapped it around her shoulders. The faintly musky smell of his body clung to its folds, and she nestled into it, breathing in the essence like a drug. It was crazy to fall in love with him, she warned herself sternly—crazy and dangerous.

But as she followed him down to the car, a voice in her head told her that common sense had absolutely nothing to do with it. She *was* falling in love with him. But if she tried to tell him that now, he would never believe her—not after she had demanded all that money as the price of being his mistress. One single tear escaped from the corner of her eyes, and trickled slowly down her cheek.

CHAPTER SEVEN

CASSY dreaded Grandpa's reaction to her news. He had spent the past fifty years hating the Claytons, convincing himself that they were responsible for all his misfortunes. He was going to be far from pleased to learn that his only granddaughter was proposing to move in with one of them.

There really was no easy way to put it, so in the end she simply announced over breakfast, 'Grandpa, I . . . I've something to tell you.' He looked up at her enquiringly. 'I'm going to live with James Clayton.'

It seemed to take several seconds for this information to make sense to him. 'Clayton? But . . . I didn't think you knew him that well,' he protested.

'I met him in New York,' she explained with minimal regard for the truth.

'I see. And what, exactly, do you mean by "going to live" with him?'

She took a deep breath. 'I'm going to move up to the Big House,' she stated flatly.

'And are you going to marry him?' he demanded from under beetling brows.

She essayed a light laugh. 'No, of course not. Don't be so old-fashioned, Grandpa.'

He glared at her indignantly. 'Old-fashioned, is it? Well, I can't help that. In my day, young people were brought up to a sense of responsibility. I don't like all these modern ways.'

'Oh, Grandpa—everyone does it these days,' she coaxed him.

'Do they indeed? Well, you aren't "everyone". You're a Durward—I *would* have hoped that you'd remember that. And to throw yourself away on a *Clayton*! Don't you think you might have some consideration for *my* feelings? After everything his grandfather did . . .?'

Cassy smiled wryly. 'Grandpa, don't you think it's time you stopped telling me fairy-stories?' she asked. He blinked at her in astonishment. 'Giles Clayton didn't cheat you, did he?' she insisted gently. 'You lost the money yourself, gambling.'

He drew himself up in righteous indignation. 'I suppose Clayton's been telling you that?' he demanded.

'Yes, he has. And it's true, isn't it, Grandpa?'

'Well, of all the outrageous . . .' he began to bluster. But he couldn't meet her level gaze, and all at once his shoulders seemed to slump. 'Yes . . . yes, it's true. It was the gambling.' He put up his hand to the corner of his eye in that dear, familiar gesture, and seemed almost surprised to find that there was a real tear there. 'I only started out to recoup what my trustees had lost me,' he told her. 'I know it was stupid of me, but somehow I couldn't seem to stop. Even when I lost . . .'

'Oh, Grandpa!' She ran round to him, and sank to her knees beside his chair, taking his thin old hands in hers. 'Why did you lie to me—all these years?'

He shook his head sadly. 'You were my little girl —my little blue-eyed girl. I couldn't bear to spoil your dreams. And now I've got myself into a terrible mess,' he added, his voice breaking. 'I owe money to Michael, Cassy dear. I thought . . . I hoped you would like him, and maybe . . .'

'Grandpa, you don't have to worry,' she promised him. 'I . . . I've spoken to James about it, and . . . he's going to let me have the money to pay Michael back. And of course he won't evict you from the house.'

He looked down at her in surprise. 'But . . . it's an awful lot of money, Cassy,' he protested.

'I know—Michael told me about it. He . . . he wanted me to marry him, but I had to say no. Well, after all, I'm in love with James.' Her voice was shaking as she said it—she had been trying for a light, matter-of-fact sort of tone, but it hadn't quite come off.

'Well,' mused Grandpa. 'I suppose he must be quite serious about you if he's prepared to be as generous as that. I can't say that I like it, but as you say, everyone's doing it these days. And whatever my little girl's set her heart on . . .' He stroked his hand down over her hair. 'I just wouldn't want you to get hurt,' he explained wistfully.

She gazed up at him through eyes misted with tears. 'Don't worry, Grandpa. Everything will be all right, I promise. But you mustn't borrow any more money from Michael. Promise?'

'Oh, yes, of course,' he assured her without hesitation. 'It was only . . . But I've learned my lesson, you know. It's taken me a long time, but from now on there'll be no more horses. I can't afford it, anyway,' he added with a shaking laugh. 'I've had to sell out my share in the syndicate, you know. And I'll probably have to let the car go. But I'll get by—I've got my old-age pension . . .'

'But what about Fishy and Jenkins?' she asked anxiously. 'How are you going to pay their wages?'

'Oh, we'll just carry on as we are—they get their pensions too now.'

'You mean—Grandpa, aren't you even *paying* them?'

He gazed back at her with wide-eyed innocence. 'Of course not. They don't need it. I told you, they get their old-age pensions . . .'

She sat back on her heels, laughing at his sheer gall. 'Oh, Grandpa! Only you could think like that!'

'Well, what's wrong with it?' he protested. 'They get more than enough to manage on, living here rent-free. We all chip in together . . .'

'And they wait on you hand and foot! Oh, Grandpa, you're impossible!'

Fishy was much more outspoken in her condemnation. '*Live* with him? Without getting married? I never thought I'd live to see the day.'

'Oh, Fishy . . .'

The housekeeper drew up with dignity. 'Don't "Oh, Fishy" me. You're not my Cassy. You're a stranger to me. Get out of my kitchen—and don't come back until you've got a ring on your finger, like a respectable woman.'

Cassy stared at her in horror. 'Fishy, please.'

But Fishy had turned her back on her, and dunked her hands into the steaming washing-up bowl. Cassy retreated from the kitchen, and escaped to her room, to sit on the window-seat hugging her knees, her heart aching with pain. Fishy had been like a mother to her for years, and her disapproval was the hardest thing of all to take.

And of course Fishy's reaction was exactly what she would get from most of the local people, too. Oh, they would probably show her a smiling face, but behind her back there would be whispers, and gradually she would find that she was a social outcast. Fundamentally, they were very conservative people.

Her only satisfaction was in being able to write the cheque to Michael, with an acidly polite covering letter. But as she walked back from the post office after dropping it into the box, her stomach was knotting with tension. Her bag was packed. James would be sending his car for her—he was expecting her for dinner.

She had been into Bath and bought a couple of new dresses—James would be expecting her to have made some effort to look nice. The one she chose to wear first was a vibrant scarlet—she felt somehow that it suited her new position in life. Fluted layers of delicate chiffon drifted from narrow shoulder-straps to her feet, clad in gold sandals; her toe-nails were painted scarlet too.

When she was dressed, she surveyed herself critically in the mirror. 'Well, you certainly look the part,' she told herself wryly. She had arranged her hair so that it fell in a cascade of curls over one shoulder, and her make-up was a work of art. 'Forty grand?' She put her hands on her hips, pouting her lips and striking a provocative pose. 'Peanuts!'

But her brave words did little to boost her courage—inside she was quaking. Tonight was the first night of the rest of her life, and nothing was ever going to be quite the same again. Oh, she had taken the necessary precautions—a mistress was not supposed to get pregnant—but her apprehension was not only about the physical aspects of the relationship she was about to embark upon.

She had already fallen in love with him. It was like an ache in her heart, always there. How much worse was it going to be, living with him, sharing his bed? And afterwards—when he had finished with her? Nothing was worse than a mistress who didn't know how to accept the end of an affair with dignity.

The peal of the doorbell jangled her nerves. Greening was here! With a last glance around her little pink and white bedroom she picked up her suitcase and went out, closing the door. She couldn't let any tears fall now—they would ruin her make-up.

Jenkins was in the hall, loftily ignoring Greening, who was standing on the doorstep like a harbinger of doom. She gave the chauffeur her suitcase. 'I . . . I'm just going to say goodnight to Grandpa,' she told him. 'I won't be a minute.'

Grandpa was ensconced in his usual chair in his sitting-room at the back of the house, a glass of brandy in his hand. The television was switched on, but he didn't seem to be watching it. He seemed to be dozing. She stood for a minute on the threshold, looking at him fondly. She couldn't find it in her heart to be angry with him, though it was his folly that had brought her to this.

'Grandpa,' she called softly. He opened his eyes. 'I'm going now. I'll come down and see you tomorrow.'

Oh . . . Yes, all right, if you like. I'll be here—I can't afford the petrol to go anywhere.'

Dear Grandpa—his own discomforts always

loomed larger in his mind than all the troubles of the rest of the world. But this evening she was grateful for that—at least he wasn't condemning her. She bent and kissed him on the cheek. 'Goodnight, Grandpa.'

'Goodnight.' He patted her hand absent-mindedly. 'Mind how you go.'

She laughed gently. 'I will,' she promised.

As she closed the sitting-room door behind her she hesitated, glancing towards the stairs that led down to the kitchen. She longed to go and say goodbye to Fishy, but she couldn't face the reproach in those sad old eyes. She turned to Jenkins, who was still standing at the door.

'Well . . . I'll be seeing you soon, Jenkins,' she said, trying to smile.

'No doubt, miss.'

'You're not going to forgive me for this either, are you, Jenkins?' she asked him, sadness in her voice.

'Your private life is entirely your own concern, miss,' he responded stiffly.

'Then kiss me goodbye, like you used to when I was little,' she begged. 'Please, Jenkins.'

He thawed slowly but at last a smile flickered over his thin face. 'All right. Goodbye, Miss Cassy.' He kissed her cheek. 'And good luck.'

She had to swallow the constriction in her throat before she could answer. 'Goodbye, Jenkins. And thank you,' she whispered.

Greening was waiting by the Rolls, holding the door open for her. As she stepped inside she took a last glance back over her shoulder at the house. It was strange—she was going barely a quarter of a mile up the road, but she felt as if she were moving away—further and more irrevocably than her move to New York.

The drive was all too short. The car turned in through the big wrought-iron gates and purred through the shadow beneath the trees. Cassy gazed out of the window at the house as they approached it. The silvery glow of the moonlight lent it a dream-like quality.

James came down the steps to greet her. He too had chosen to honour the occasion with formal dress—black dinner-jacket, white bow-tie. He opened the car door, and held out an imperious hand. She placed hers in it, and stepped out into the cool night air.

The smile that curved his hard mouth did nothing to warm the obsidian darkness of his eyes. 'Good evening, my dear,' he purred. 'I'm glad you came.'

'I could hardly do anything else, could I?' she retorted, nervousness lending a sharp edge to her voice.

'You've had your money,' he pointed out.

'Yes. But you're still holding an eviction notice over my head,' she reminded him icily. 'Can we go inside? It's cold out here.'

'By all means. Greening will take your luggage up to your room, and a maid will unpack it for you.'

'*My* room?'

'It's next to mine,' he told her, his smile taking on a sardonic quality. 'There's a connecting door.'

'I see.'

'But there isn't a key.'

'I wasn't going to ask for one,' she informed him with lofty dignity. 'I know better than to waste my breath.'

'I'm glad to hear it.' They crossed the hall to the small drawing-room. 'Would you like a drink before dinner?' James enquired with a formal politeness that was really almost absurd under the circumstances. But she was grateful that he was not rushing to bring the evening to its ultimate conclusion, giving her a little time to adjust.

She accepted a drink with a reasonable semblance of composure, and sat down in one of the deep, comfortable armchairs. She had seen a little of this room during the party. It was nothing like as grand as the main drawing-room. The floor was covered with a good Aubusson carpet, and the furniture was upholstered in wine-red velvet. The only really valuable piece in here was a long-case clock, still keeping excellent time though it was probably nearly three hundred years old.

'You're admiring the clock,' commented James as he brought her drink.

'Yes. Where did you get it?'

'It came with the house. I dare say it even predates the alterations. I've been given 1705 on it.'

'Really? Who's it by?'

'Tompion and Banger. The wood is chestnut.'

'I thought it was unusual. It must be worth a great deal.'

'Slightly more than I paid for you, my dear,' he returned tauntingly.

Cassy flushed, and looked away quickly. He had mixed her martini very dry, the American way, and she sipped it sparingly. Suddenly there was a patter of feet in the corridor, and she glanced round to see the two Weimaraners standing hopefully in the doorway.

'Do you like dogs?' James asked her.

'Of course.'

'Come then,' he called to the dogs. They bounced at once into the room, going first for a pat from their master, and then turning to look at Cassy with intelligent amber eyes. 'This is Donner, and this one's Blitzen,' he introduced them.

Blitzen hung back, uncertain, but Donner walked over to Cassy, sniffed at her knees for a moment, and then sat down, expecting a stroke. Cassy ran her hand over the finely chiselled head. 'Well, aren't you beautiful?' she murmured. The dog rubbed his cheek luxuriously against Cassy's hand.

James laughed. 'Oh, he'll have you doing for hours,' he warned her. 'Go on, the pair of you. You've said hello. Back to quarters. Mrs Bolliver will tell me off if she finds your hairs all over the carpet tomorrow.'

Cassy slanted him a curious glance from beneath her lashes as the dogs trotted obediently away. For a fleeting moment she seemed to have glimpsed a different person from the one she thought she knew—one who could speak with a warm laugh in his voice and who could shed his cynicism to mock himself gently.

But before she could be sure of the impression there was another footfall behind her, and the young butler's voice announced, 'Dinner is served, sir.'

'Thank you, Coleman. Shall we go through, Cassy?'

The dining-room was on the north-west corner of the house, corresponding in position to the library, which was on the north-east, and of the same proportions. The long rosewood dining-table would easily seat twenty, but tonight it was laid only for two, with a spotless white linen cloth across the centre, lit by the soft glow of candles from two silver candelabra set on each side.

James helped her to her seat, and then walked round to the other side of the table. As Coleman, James's young butler, served her with a bowl of clear watercress soup she glanced across at him enquiringly. 'This is very grand,' she observed drily. 'Do you always dine in here?'

'Usually,' he responded with no trace of diffidence. 'It's no more trouble than to eat in the breakfast-room.'

The butler withdrew, and she sipped her soup in silence. She wasn't at all hungry—there was too much tension inside her, knotting her stomach. She watched James covertly from beneath her lashes, wondering if he felt it too. He seemed to be fully in control, his handsome, slightly aquiline features softened a little by the flickering candlelight.

For a moment she wondered if she could tell him the truth about why she had wanted the money— maybe then he would realise that she wasn't the mercenary bitch he thought her. She could even tell him . . . No, she couldn't. He wasn't interested in whether or not she loved him—he wanted an obliging mistress, not a clinging lover. She would keep her secrets.

Coleman returned to remove the soup bowls, and serve the main course. 'This is our own trout,' James told her. 'Caught fresh this morning, in the lake.'

'*You* caught it?' she enquired, surprised.

He nodded. 'There's nothing I like better than a couple of hours' fishing early in the morning. It's very relaxing.'

'I'm surprised you can find the time.'

'I'm afraid I can't as often as I would like. I have to travel abroad a great deal. But I've got a terminal of our main-frame computer installed down here now, so when I can I try to work from home.'

'I see. And . . . will you be taking me with you when you go abroad?' she asked.

'Not usually. You'd get bored—they're only business trips.'

She fell silent again, toying with her fish. She was too nervous to have much of an appetite, but she drank rather a lot of the wine, deliberately seeking the artificial aid of the alcohol to help her relax.

'Shall I send for another bottle?' enquired James, an inflection of ironic humour in his voice.

'Oh . . . no, that will do,' she answered quickly, noticing with surprise that the bottle was empty.

He turned the label away from her. 'Come on then,' he challenged teasingly. 'Tell me what it is.'

She laughed, and closed her eyes to concentrate on the lingering flavour. It was a well balanced wine, the fresh acidity of the Chardonnay grape mellowed by a subtle hint of wood-age . . . 'It's a Burgundy,' she suggested.

'Easy!'

'A good year. Is it a Meursault?'

'No.'

She opened her eyes and reached for the bottle. 'A Montrachet,' she cried. 'Oh, I should have guessed!'

'Yes, you should. It's reassuring to know that even an expert can make a mistake occasionally.'

'I told you, I'm not an expert. Oh, lovely—orange sorbet,' she added as Coleman brought in the dessert. 'I love the way they do them like this, in the actual orange peel. I tried it once, but it went all wonky.'

'Did it really?' he asked, warm laughter in his voice. 'I expect it's the sort of thing that takes a lot of practice.'

'Mmm,' she nodded as she took her first spoonful, and let it melt on her tongue. 'It's delicious. Your cook must be brilliant!'

'Quite a genius. You're going to make yourself very popular with her if you're so generous with your praise.'

'You must keep quite a big staff here,' she remarked curiously.

'Only Coleman and Mrs Bolliver live in,' he told her. 'The rest are daily.'

'Oh, I see. You're very lucky—it's such a lovely house.'

He smiled, lifting one eyebrow enquiringly. 'Am I forgiven for owning it, then?'

'Oh, I suppose so,' she conceded, returning the smile. 'I'm just glad it hasn't been turned into a health-farm, or an amusement park.'

He laughed aloud. 'Heaven forbid! Would you like another look round when you've finished your meal?'

'Oh, yes, please,' she agreed eagerly. The wine had done its work. She was still a little nervous, but a reckless spirit was growing inside her. She had stepped on to a fairground ride, and she couldn't get off until the ride was finished.

The butler brought coffee, and they chatted in quite a friendly way while they drank it, and then

James said, 'Well, if you're ready. The Grand Tour.'

'Right.' Boldly she put her hand on his arm, and they left the dining-room.

'The servants' quarters are through there,' he told her, nodding towards a door at the end of the corridor. 'This is the breakfast-room.' He opened another door, opposite the dining-room, to show her a small, pleasant room overlooking the gardens. 'I sometimes dine in there in the summer—it's nice with the windows open, looking down over the valley and watching the sunset.'

'It sounds fabulous,' she breathed.

'And of course, this is the small drawing-room,' he went on as they passed the door to the room with the long-case clock. The dogs appeared again from a door on their left. 'That's just a kind of cloakroom,' James told her.

'Do the dogs have the run of the house?' she asked him.

'More or less. They're guard dogs, as well as pets. But they don't usually go in the main rooms, of course.' He paused by the wide glass doors that led into the huge main drawing-room. 'I don't use this room a great deal, except for entertaining,' he went on.

'Oh, that's a shame,' she protested, walking through it towards the generous curve of the french windows. 'The view is wonderful from here.'

'I know. But it's such a big room—you almost need to use a telephone to have a conversation from one end of it to the other.'

She laughed up at him—and her heart suddenly thudded as she realised how close he was standing to her. She lowered her eyes in swift defensiveness,

and moved away. 'This chimney-piece must be by
Adam,' she observed, walking over to it.

'Wrong again. It's by Richard Westmacott.' He
was letting her keep her distance, strolling along
with his hands in his pockets as she drifted round
the room, examining the furniture, which was
mostly French of the Louis XVI period.

The next room was the billiard-room. James
switched on the light that hung low over the table,
and picked up the cue. 'Have you ever played?' he
asked her.

'I've played a little pool in America.'

'Oh, pool,' he mocked scornfully. 'There's no
skill in that.'

'Yes, there is,' she protested indignantly. 'It's a
matter of tactics.'

'Rubbish. If you can pot the ball, you can win
every time. And the table's so small that if you've
got any sort of straight aim, you can't miss.'

'That isn't true,' she insisted.

'Come on then, Steve Davis,' he challenged
teasingly. 'Let's see you pot the ball on this table.'
He handed her the cue. 'Here, I'll line them up for
you.' He put one of the red balls near the centre
pocket, and the white in an easy position some
eighteen inches away from it.

'That's a piece of cake,' she declared confidently, bending to line up her shot. But as she
looked along the length of the cue, she realised that
she had been a little over-optimistic. The table was
much larger than a pool table, and the pocket
looked an awfully long way away. She swung her
cuing arm, trying to relax the elbow, and then,
biting her tongue with concentration, she took her
shot. She missed by more than six inches.

'A piece of cake?' laughed James. 'You were a mile out!'

'No, I wasn't,' she retorted. 'I'm just not used to the run of the table.'

'Go on then, try another shot.'

He lined the balls up for her again, making it even easier this time, but she missed again, though she managed to get the ball into the jaws of the pocket. She took a second shot, and sank it.

'There!' she cried triumphantly. 'How's that?'

'Not bad. You need to hold your elbow up just a little higher.' He came round behind her, and bent with her over the table, correcting her position. 'Relax your arm,' he coaxed.

She felt like laughing aloud. Relax? With him leaning over her like this, his hands touching her bare shoulders, his breath warm against her hair? Her senses were reeling, her legs felt weak. She shouldn't have drunk all that wine. She took the shot wildly. The ball skipped, bounced over the far cushion, and rolled away across the floor.

James roared with laughter. 'What on earth was that supposed to be?'

She turned to him, laughing too. He was still very close. Their eyes met . . . and the laughing stopped. He took the cue from her nerveless fingers, and laid it across the table as he came closer, so that she had to lean back as his eyes still held hers with that strange, powerful compulsion.

His hands slid slowly up her arms to grip her shoulders. She had started to tremble, recognising the dark intent in his eyes. He came closer still, trapping her against the table so that her whole body was curved vulnerably against his. She could feel the warning tension of male arousal in him.

Her time had run out. His eyes were burning as they gazed down into hers. 'At last,' he murmured, his voice a husky growl.

Her breath was warm on her lips as his head bent towards hers. His mouth claimed hers with hungry possessiveness, and his kiss swirled her into a dangerous land, where she could only follow him blindly. His tongue plundered deep into the sweet, defenceless valley of her mouth, demanding her total surrender, and she yielded all that he asked and more.

Her heart was pounding so fast that she felt dizzy, and she barely realised that he had scooped her up in his arms and was carrying her towards the door. The deep, feminine core of her responded helplessly to that masculine strength, and she clung to him as he carried her straight up the stairs and pushed open the door of his bedroom.

The room was lit by the soft glow of a lamp, and by its warm light she saw a large room, Jacobean in style, panelled from floor to ceiling with gleaming oak. Dominating the room was a huge four-poster bed. It was just how she had imagined it would look.

He set her on her feet in the middle of the room. Her sandals had slipped off somewhere on the stairs and she had to stretch up on tiptoe as he drew her up in his arms again, and his mouth closed over hers in a tender, sensuous kiss that swept away the last shreds of her sanity.

Very slowly he drew down the zip of her dress. Heat shimmered through her as she felt the silky fabric fall away from her body. He let it drop to the floor, and then picked it up and tossed it over a chair, and she stood with lowered eyes as he turned back to her.

She had splashed out on the best underwear she could afford—a dainty wisp of delicate creamy-white French silk, lavishly trimmed with lace—and she had opted for stockings and suspenders instead of tights. He came towards her slowly, and she stood waiting for him, trembling.

He put out his hands, and brushed the straps of her silk teddy from her shoulders. It slid slowly to the floor, leaving her naked except for the tiny suspender belt and pale silk stockings. She heard him draw in his breath, and couldn't resist a cautious peep at him from beneath her lashes. The unbridled desire she saw in his eyes took her breath away.

'This really is your first time, isn't it?' he asked gently. She nodded, far beyond the power of speech. 'Don't worry,' he murmured. 'It'll be all right.'

He picked her up again, and carried her over to the bed. She wrapped her arms around his neck, and drew him down with her, shivering as she felt the brush of his cotton shirt against her bare breasts. His flesh felt hot through his clothes, and she wondered fleetingly how hers felt to him.

His hands began to stroke slowly over her body, savouring every curve, and she stretched languorously like a cat, wantonly inviting his caresses. Every touch was gentle and arousing, leading her along paths of sensuality of which he was master. She felt just a faint twinge of jealousy of all the other women who had gone before her and would come after, but she forced it into the back of her mind.

His touch was light, tantalising her, torturing

her, as he traced lazy circles over her aching breasts with his fingertips, smiling as the tender pink nipples puckered in exquisite response. She moaned softly, her spine twisting and curling with ecstasy as he teased the sweetly sensitive buds, the pleasure shafting into her brain like incandescent wires.

Her head tipped back as she gasped for air. James's kisses were scalding her face, swirling over the delicate shell of her ear, trailing fire down into the sensitive hollow of her shoulder. His cheek rasped against her silken skin, and a surge of exquisite pleasure rippled through her as his hot mouth found the tender bud of her nipple and began to suckle.

Instinctively she reached out and began to tug at his shirt, longing for the feel of his naked skin against hers. He laughed, low in his throat, and standing up he quickly stripped off his clothes. She watched him, her heartbeat accelerating at the sight of those hard muscles moving smoothly beneath his golden skin, the smattering of dark curls across his wide chest.

She reached out and drew him down to her, her mouth seeking hungrily for his kiss. He stretched out beside her on the bed, cradling her in his arms as his mouth melted over hers, his tongue sweeping languorously into every secret corner, while his hand caressed her body with gentle possessiveness.

She lay back against the pillows, yielding willingly as he coaxed apart her slender thighs, quivering at the touch of his fingers as he sought the most intimate caresses. She seemed to be melting in a flood of sensuous warmth, floating on a soft cloud, swirling in a land of mysterious darkness.

She gasped as he took her, opening startled eyes to find him smiling down at her. 'I'm sorry—I didn't mean to hurt you,' he coaxed. 'Just relax . . . take it nice and easy . . .'

She could only submit as he took his pleasure, her body surrendering totally to his. But there was a deep satisfaction in that, a glow that spread slowly from the pit of her stomach until it reached every part of her. She moved with him, feeling the pounding beat of his heart close to her own, until one last violent tremor shook him, and with a groan he fell into her arms, almost crushing her beneath his weight.

She held him tightly, stroking his hair, staring up at the elaborately carved tester of the bed with unseeing eyes. She never wanted to move from this spot, never wanted to let him go.

CHAPTER EIGHT

'DON'T you think it's time we got up?'

James stretched luxuriously on the pillows. 'No. Why should we?'

'Well, for one thing, because it's gone half past nine. Don't you have a vast international business empire to run?'

'It can run itself for a little while,' he declared lazily. 'I'm going to keep you here in bed, and have my wicked way with you.'

Cassy giggled. 'You've been having your wicked way all night,' she reminded him, her cheeks faintly pink at the memory.

'Mmm.' He bundled her into his arms, and nuzzled into the hollow of her shoulder. 'And I'm going to do it again.'

She really had no objections whatsoever to that idea, and participated with a willingness that more than made up for her lack of expertise. But afterwards he glanced at the clock, and groaned. 'Ah well, I suppose I *must* get up.' He levered himself up off the bed, and smiled down at her. 'We can go riding later, if you like.'

'Oh yes, that would be nice,' she agreed readily.

'After lunch, OK? See you later.' He bent and dropped a kiss on her forehead, and then vanished into his dressing-room.

She lay back on the pillows, and closed her eyes. Whatever she had imagined it was going to be like, the reality had come as a total surprise. She stretched deliciously as she relived the memories. It had been a fabulous night—laughing one minute, drowning in passion the next. So many times it had been on her lips to tell him that she was really in love with him, but each time she had checked herself. He wasn't going to believe her, and she couldn't bear to get a cynical answer from him.

That thought punctured the bubble of happiness inside her, and it deflated like a leftover balloon. She opened her eyes again, and glanced around the room. On the bedside table were the remains of their breakfast, brought in an hour earlier by the butler. He had seemed to treat her presence as a completely normal occurrence, and she wondered how often he served breakfast in bed to James and a lady-friend.

She ought to get up—not that there was any particular hurry, she had nothing to do until lunch time. It was an unusual position for her to be in. It wasn't even as if she could do anything around the house—it wasn't her house. And James would be busy, so she would be on her own.

She could go and see Grandpa, of course—she had been going to go this afternoon, after their ride, but with luck James might be free again then, so they could spend the time together. She got out of bed, and wrapped herself up in James's black silk kimono, and picking up her clothes from where they had been discarded the previous night she pushed open the connecting door and went into her room.

It seemed odd to call it 'her' room—it had nothing of hers in it at all. All her clothes had been hung away neatly in the dressing-room by an unseen maid. It was like a hotel room—albeit a very luxurious one. Like James's room, it overlooked the gardens and the lake. But in style it was pure Regency, with silk-striped wallpaper of palest cream, and elegantly draped almond-green velvet curtains. The furniture was gracefully carved— who had chosen it? One of her predecessors?

She didn't know much about the details of James's private life over the past few years. She had heard names mentioned from time to time by the gossips in the village, but they had meant nothing to her then. She cast her mind back to the night of the party. There had been plenty of beautiful women there—any of them could have been his 'exes'. And those two women he had been with at the Mermaid—who were they?

Impatiently she shook her head, and walked over to the bathroom. It was stupid to let herself think about the others—it only made her miserable. Better to live only in the present. She hugged his kimono around her body, and started to run herself a bath.

A tap on the door made her look up in surprise. 'Come in,' she called uncertainly. The door opened, and she found herself looking at the familiar face of one of her old childhood friends from the village. 'Carol!' she exclaimed, smiling in delight. 'What on earth are you doing here?'

There was no answering smile. 'I work here,' was the blunt response.

'Oh . . .' Cassy hesitated, feeling herself beginning to blush. 'Was it you who put my things away?' she asked.

'Yes, miss.'

She laughed nervously. 'Oh, heavens, Carol, don't

call me "miss",' she pleaded. 'I mean . . .
remember when we used to play jumping the
stream, and Janet Wilson fell in and her shoes got
stuck in the mud?'

'Yes, miss.'

'What . . . what's Janet doing now?' She tried to
make her voice sound breezy and cheerful.

'She'm married, miss.'

'Oh . . . that's nice. And . . . and what about
you? How have you been?'

'I'm engaged, miss.'

'Oh really? Who to?'

'You wouldn't know him, miss. He'm from
Bristol. I came up to see if there was anything you
wanted. I always wait on the ladies as use this
room,' she added significantly.

'Oh . . . I see.' Cassy felt defeated. 'Well, I . . .
There's nothing I want at the moment, thank you,'
she stammered.

'Shall I finish running your bath, miss?'

'Thank you.'

While the girl fussed in the bathroom, Cassy
wandered over to the window and stood staring
bleakly out at the swans on the lake. She had
handled that situation very badly—it had been
embarrassing for both of them. It would probably
have been much easier if she had really been
mistress of the house, but her present position was
ambiguous. She wasn't exactly a guest, but she
didn't quite belong. She was just one of the 'ladies'
who used this room.

Tears of humiliation sprang to her eyes. Carol
had made her opinion of her quite plain—and she
had once been a friend. The same experience was
going to be repeated over and over down in the

village. If she had been an outsider, she probably wouldn't be judged so harshly. But she was one of their own, and she had turned her back on respectability to live 'in sin'.

'Your bath is ready, miss,' came Carol's deadpan voice behind her. 'Sir James has lunch at one o'clock.'

'Thank you, Carol.' She managed to inject a little dignity into her voice.

'Will that be all, miss?'

'Yes, thank you.'

She was glad when the door closed behind her. She stripped off the kimono, and sank gratefully into the warm water. Life was going to be very strange—there would be a lot of adjustments to be made. What was it James had said—she would have nothing to do but look beautiful? Just be a pretty toy, waiting on his convenience, serving his pleasure—until he got bored with her. And then what? If he was feeling generous, he would grant her the lease on Grandpa's house—a bone tossed to an obedient dog.

In a spurt of anger she slapped the surface of the water with the flat of her hands, making it splash up over the sides of the bath. Dammit, she didn't *want* to sit around all day filing her nails and choosing what dress to wear for dinner. She had had a career for six years—a challenging, exciting career that had demanded drive, intelligence, ambition. How could she become a different person overnight? It just wasn't fair. James had everything, and she had nothing. She had to find something to do.

After her bath, as she had planned, she went down to see Grandpa, using the short cut through the wicket-gate and the rough path down to his garden. She was going to slip in through the back door and go straight upstairs, shy of bumping into Fishy, but as she crossed the scullery she heard the housekeepers's voice.

'Well, something will have to be done. I tell you, this house is a death-trap. That's the third time this week I've had a shock off that switch.'

'It's the damp,' Jenkins responded lugubriously. 'It's not worth having the re-wiring done unless something's done about the damp as well, or in no time at all you'll just be back where you started.'

Cassy pushed open the door, and hesitated on the threshold. 'I—I'm sorry,' she began tentatively. 'I couldn't help hearing you—I've just come down to see Grandpa.'

Fishy heaved herself up with massive dignity, and stalked into the pantry without saying a word. Cassy gazed bleakly at her retreating back. She was still beyond the pale.

But Jenkins smiled, and came over to her, shutting the kitchen door discreetly behind him. 'Don't mind it,' he said quietly. 'She'll come round.'

'I hope so. What was that about the wiring, Jenkins? Is it really getting dangerous?'

He nodded. 'I'm afraid so. The whole lot fused a couple of weeks ago. It's more than fifty years old, mind. It needs stripping out completely, and re-doing.'

'And the damp-course too?'

'Yes. There's a lot more than that besides—the roof, for one.

'I couldn't afford a new roof,' she said. 'But I could get the wiring and the damp-course done.'

'That'd be a help, Miss Cassy. I despair in the winter—one of these days the whole house will just go up in flames.'

'Oh, no! We can't have that. And another thing, Jenkins. I don't like to mention it to Fishy—well, I can't at the moment anyway—but I was thinking about getting a girl in from the village to help out, just with the heavy work.'

He smiled. 'That's a good idea, miss. Mrs Fisher *is* finding it a bit much—well, we're none of us getting any younger. You leave it to me. There's Betty Taylor's girl as would be ideal—not bright, but a good little worker and does as she's told. I'll put Mrs Fisher in the way of thinking it was her own idea.'

'Thank you, Jenkins. And . . . and if she wants to know where I've got the money to pay for it, tell her . . . tell her . . .'

'Well, naturally you've got some savings, miss,' Jenkins supplied helpfully. 'And a credit to you it is to be using them to help your own, as Mrs Fisher will appreciate.'

'Oh, I don't want her to think I'm trying to buy her favour . . .'

'She'll think nothing of the kind. Now you run along upstairs and see your Grandpa. He needs a bit of cheering up.'

'What have you been doing this morning?' asked James over lunch.

'Oh, I went down to see Grandpa,' she told him.

'Yes? How is he?'

'Having one of his grumps,' she admitted ruefully.

'Lost on the horses again?'

She flashed him a cold look. 'He's given up gambling.'

He laughed scornfully. 'That'll be the day.'

'What's getting him down is the state of the house,' she said, turning the subject to what she wanted to discuss. 'It needs a lot of work doing to it.'

'I'm quite aware of that,' he returned coolly. 'I'm also aware of who let it get into the state it's in.'

'Yes, well . . . the condition of the wiring is very dangerous,' she ploughed on. 'And the damp-proof course needs replacing . . .'

'And you're expecting me to have them done?'

'No, I'm not,' she retorted indignantly. 'I'll pay for it.'

'Oh?' He lifted one sardonic eyebrow. 'You haven't spent the whole of that forty thousand yet then?'

'I can afford it, she asserted.

'Then go ahead and get it done.'

'Right. I . . . I'm also going to hire young Mandy Taylor from the village to help out with the housework.'

'What you do about your grandfather is entirely up to you,' he said.

'Yes, but I . . . I'm going to need to get a job myself . . .'

'I told you, I'll give you an allowance. I think you'll find that it's more than enough to pay for little Mandy's services, as well as all your frippery.' The glint in his eyes warned her that the subject was closed, and she could do nothing but swallow her gall. It ruined the taste of the delicious lunch his cook had prepared, but she had to make herself smile, and converse pleasantly with him. He held too much power over her, in every way—she had to do exactly as he wanted.

She wasn't entirely sorry when he told her that he wouldn't be able to come riding with her after all—something had cropped up in Spain, and he had to wait for an urgent telephone call. 'Norton will go out with you,' he said. 'I've told him to saddle you up a young filly I've got—her name's Topaz. She can be a little fidgety—she needs a light hand, but let her know who's boss.'

'It's a long time since I've ridden,' she reminded him doubtfully.

'You'll be OK,' he assured her easily. 'You used to be one of the best little riders in the county, and you won't have forgotten.'

She was pleased at the throw-away compliment—more pleased than she ever was by his comments about her looks. She responded warmly to his kiss, and hurried upstairs to change into the jodhpurs and riding-boots she had brought up from home.

The stable-lad brought the horse out for her. She was a handsome young bay, nice to look at, but the first time she got on her back she napped and tried to throw her off. Cassy was glad she had chosen to wear a proper riding-helmet instead of the flimsy hat favoured by the weekend hackers.

It was a lovely afternoon, and Cassy could think of no better way to spend it than riding out over the rolling Somerset hills. Norton, James's groom, came with her, exercising his big Irish hunter, Goldfinger. They hacked along the country lanes, and then turned up on to the grassy slopes to give the horses a good gallop.

By the time they got back to the stables, the horse was getting used to her, and she had little trouble controlling her desire to frisk home. But as they rode into the stable-yard she was surprised to see that James had come down to meet her. Topaz picked up her sudden agitation, and began to dance sideways. James caught the bridle, and held her steady as Cassy dismounted.

'How did you enjoy your ride?' he asked pleasantly.

'Fabulous! She tried to throw me off at first, but I think we've come to an understanding now, haven't we, girl?' The horse nuzzled against her shoulder, as if in agreement, and she stroked her nose affectionately.

'Good. I came down to tell you that I've got to pop over to Madrid.'

Suddenly the young horse began to skit around again, and Cassy had to give all her attention to calming her. 'Couldn't I come with you?' she asked him.

'It's not worth it—I'll be back tomorrow afternoon.'

The stable-lad came and took the horse back to her stable, and Cassy walked back to the house with James. 'What time are you leaving?'

'In about an hour. I hoped you wouldn't be too long on your ride,' he added, slanting her one of those sorcerer's smiles.

His intention was unmistakable, and Cassy's heart bounced. 'H . . . haven't you got to pack, or something?' she asked unsteadily.

'Carol's doing it.'

Fifty minutes later he left her lying on her bed, and

ten minutes after that she heard the door of his bedroom close, and heard his footsteps on the stairs. Dismally she got up and got dressed again. Was this what it was going to be like? Left on her own at a moment's notice, waiting until he had a few moments to spare for her? Well, after all, what could she expect? she asked herself bitterly. She was only his mistress.

As she walked down the stairs, she heard the butler's voice in the hall, speaking softly on the telephone. 'Yes, I gave him your message, Miss Julia . . . Well, I'm sorry, I'm sure he . . . Yes, Miss Julia, I'll tell him.' He put the receiver down, and turned from the telephone, a sardonic smile on his face. As he heard Cassy's footsteps on the stairs he looked up quickly, plainly embarrassed.

'Oh, miss, I'm sorry, I . . . I didn't know you were there. I . . .'

'That's all right,' she answered wryly. 'I don't suppose the call was for me anyway, was it?'

'No, miss,' he admitted, unable quite to suppress that smile.

'Who was it?' she asked tensely.

The young man looked uncomfortable. 'Just a . . . a friend of Sir James's,' he said.

'Very well. Thank you, Coleman.'

His relief at not being cross-questioned further was evident. 'Will you be dining alone this evening, miss?' he enquired politely.

She signed bleakly. 'I suppose so.'

It was lonely, dining on her own in the grand dining-room. She couldn't help wondering about that call. Julia. Who was she? One of the 'ladies' who had used that room in the past? What was she like? Pretty, no doubt. Did James always go for

blondes, or did his tastes vary? Had she lived here
with him, eaten at this grand table, slept in that
comfortable bed? And in three months, six
months, a year—would there be someone else
sitting here, and would she herself be the pathetic
voice on the other end of the telephone? 'Tell him I
called . . .'

For her own self-respect, for her very survival,
she had to find a way to retain her own identity.
Whatever James said, she needed to find a job.
When Coleman came in to remove her plate she
said to him, 'I think I'll take my coffee in the small
drawing-room. Is there a copy of the local paper?'

'Yes, miss. I'll bring it to you.'

She settled herself in one of the comfortable
armchairs, and began to comb through the situ-
ations vacant column. There wasn't really anything
that would fit the bill—it had to be local, and it had
to be part-time. She tried telephoning a couple of
them—'Nanny wanted', but she had to admit to no
experience with children, and 'Canvassers', but it
was mostly evening work—James would never
agree to that.

Dispirited, she turned to the rest of the local
news. There were several antique fairs advertised—
there were often quite a few at this time of year. It
might be interesting just to go and browse . . . Or
even . . . She sat up straight as an idea sprang full-
grown into her mind. Of course—it would be
perfect! And if she was careful, James need never
know what she was doing! She glanced at her
watch. It would only be four o'clock in New York.
She reached for the telephone again.

Rhoda sounded delighted to hear from her.
'Cassy! How are you, honey? You're not ringing to

tell me you've changed your mind about staying home, are you?'

Cassy laughed. 'No, Rhoda, I'm sorry. But I've got a proposition to put to you. You remember saying once or twice that it might be worth coming over to Europe on a buying trip?'

Rhoda caught on at once. 'Cassy! Why didn't I think of that? You're right there! I'll take everything you can send me. Craig can help us arrange the shipping . . .

'You really think it would work out?'

'Why shouldn't it? You know how big the market is over here—the sky's the limit. What I haven't got room for, I can pass along to Marsha, or even Edward Stuart. And we could make a big saving on shipping costs if we use containers.'

'Hey, hang on a minute, Rhoda!' Cassy protested. 'I shall only be working part-time, you know. And besides, I'll have to be careful I don't run into problems over export licences.'

'I'll pay you an extra five per cent on your usual commission for all the extra work involved,' Rhoda rushed on. 'Keep your eyes open for wine-coolers—I've had several enquiries recently. And Georgian silverware—especially if you can get a good provenance on it. Since that forgeries scandal people are being very careful, but that means they're all the more prepared to pay for the real thing.'

'I'll do my best.'

'And all the glass you can get.'

'Of course,' laughed Cassy. 'OK, Rhoda, I'll see what I can pick up over the next couple of weeks, and then we'll see about the best way of getting it over there.'

*   *   *

The following afternoon, James rang to say he wouldn't be home after all. Cassy was deeply disappointed—she would hardly have believed it possible that she could have missed him so much, after only one night. But it was one of the things that she was going to have to learn to accept, so she didn't complain.

'Would you mind if I borrowed one of the cars?' she asked him tentatively. 'Just to run up to Bath.'

'You want to go shopping? Help yourself—but not the Aston Martin or the Roller, please.'

She laughed. 'I wouldn't dare. I just want something to run around in.'

'Sure. Have you been to see your grandfather?'

'Yes, I popped over this morning. He's OK. They're coming on Monday to start work on the house.'

'Good. It might be worth getting the roof done while we're at it.'

'Yes.' Was he offering to pay for that himself? She didn't like to ask. Instead she asked, 'When will you be home?'

'I'm not sure. The day after tomorrow, I hope. Goodbye.'

'Goodbye, James.'

The early bird was the one that caught the worm when it came to antique fairs, so the next morning she set out a little after seven thirty to drive over to Wells. She made several purchases, including a nice early Georgian concertina card-table with cabriole legs, a fine Wheildon teapot, and a small blue bottle-vase that she was sure was by Loetz—Rhoda would probably like that so much she wouldn't be able to part with it.

The problem was, what could she do with them until she could arrange to send them over to Rhoda? She couldn't keep them at Bradley Park—she would have to keep her activities a secret from James. Maybe eventually she might be able to persuade him to let her work, but for the time being she didn't want to risk a confrontation.

The obvious thing to do was to take them to Grandpa's, so she drove straight round there. To her surprise, Michael Farrell's car was outside. She hesitated for a moment, reluctant to go in while he was there. But she had to get the stuff out of the car.

Michael had made himself at home once again, lounging on the settee in Grandpa's sitting-room, drinking his brandy. He looked up as she came in, that horribly smug smile spreading over his face when he saw her. 'Well now, look who's here,' he drawled, his voice rich with mockery. 'Good afternoon, darling. And how are you keeping?'

'Very well, thank you,' she returned coolly. 'Hello, Grandpa.'

Grandpa evaded her eyes. 'Hello, Cassy,' he murmured guiltily. 'What are you doing here?'

'I told you yesterday that I'd come over again today,' she reminded him.

'Oh. Are you staying to lunch?'

'Well, I was going to,' she said, not troubling to disguise the fact that Michael's presence had made her reconsider. 'I've brought a couple of boxes of stuff I'd like to leave upstairs for a few days.'

He didn't seem at all interested. 'Get Jenkins to give you a hand,' he suggested.

'No, it's all right—it isn't heavy.'

'I'll help you,' volunteered Michael, standing up.

'I can manage, thank you,' she responded crisply.

But he followed her out to the car. 'So,' he drawled, an unpleasant edge in his voice. 'You've moved in with Clayton then?' She ignored him. 'He won't marry you, you know,' he persisted. 'There's been plenty of pretty girls thought they could catch him on their hook, but he's managed to wriggle away from it every time.'

'I'm not expecting him to marry me,' she retorted crisply.

'Ah, well that's all right then, isn't it?' he sneered. 'Mind, I'd have thought you'd have struck a better bargain—I had you down for an intelligent woman. You've sold yourself cheap.'

She opened the boot of the car, and took out the cardboard box she had packed the smaller items into. She turned back to the house, stalking past Michael with her head in the air.

'I'll fetch this little table for you then, shall I?' he offered.

'Thank you.'

He followed her back into the house, and upstairs to her room. She put the things in a corner out of the way, and turned again to find Michael browsing around the room.

'Nice house, this,' he remarked. 'Has Clayton signed the deeds over to you, then?'

'That's none of your business,' she snapped defensively.

He laughed knowingly. 'Meaning he hasn't. Well, my offer still stands, you know. I'm prepared to overlook the fact that the goods are a little . . . shop-soiled.'

The anger inside her was like a ball of cold lead. 'Let me tell you something, Mr Farrell,' she enunicated in frigid tones. 'You are without doubt the nastiest little man I have ever met in my life. If you were bleeding to death in the gutter I wouldn't even bother to spit on you. I wouldn't marry you if the alternative was to spend the rest of my life scrubbing out cess-pits. Do I make myself clear?'

His gimlet eyes blazed in fury. 'Perfectly, Miss Durward,' he returned, a quiet menace in his voice. 'But you're going to regret this—I promise you that.' He turned sharply on his heel and walked out of the room, leaving her trembling with reaction.

CHAPTER NINE

To Cassy's relief, Michael didn't stay for lunch. She ate with Grandpa, who was still too bound up with his own interests to take much notice of her problems. There would be no help forthcoming from that quarter, she reflected ruefully as she drove back up to the Big House. She was on her own.

She left the car in the garage next to the stables, and walked up to the house, deep in thought. It wasn't going to be easy to keep her activities from James—he would want to know why she was going out so early in the morning. She would have to think of some excuse.

'Hello, there. Where have you been?'

She started guiltily at the sound of James's voice. He was standing in the doorway of his business-room, leaning against the frame. 'Oh, I .. . I went down to Grandpa's for lunch,' she answered quickly.

'In the car?' He smiled teasingly. 'You're getting lazy.'

'Oh . . . no, I went for a drive first. To Bath.'

'Buy anything?' he asked in a friendly tone.

She shrugged. 'No, I was only window-shopping. When did you get back?'

'About ten o'clock.'

'Oh, I'm sorry I wasn't here. I wasn't expecting you back until tomorrow.' She was trying to speak lightly, but her heart was beginning to race. It was the way he looked at her.

'I had a good reason to hurry back,' he told her, walking slowly towards her, his dark eyes drifting down over her, his intention unmistakable. 'I brought you a present.'

'D—did you?'

'You didn't think I'd forget, did you? Hold out your hand.'

She did as she was bid, and he put into her hand a fan. She gasped in delight. It was lovely—the leaf was of fine chicken-skin, painted in delicate colours, and the ribs were ivory.

'Do you like it?'

'Of course. It's beautiful. Thank you—thank you very much.' Her eyes searched his. He had taken the trouble, in the middle of his business trip, to choose a present for her!

'Are you riding this afternoon?' he asked her.

'Oh, yes, if you want to.'

'Right. In half an hour?'

'OK.'

She went up to her room, and changed into her light jodhpurs and a white cotton shirt. She coiled her hair up on to the crown of her head, and pulled on her green riding-boots. Then she wandered over to the dressing-table, and picked up the fan again. It was a very pretty little thing—probably eighteenth century. A small smile curved her delicate mouth. In the middle of his business trip, he'd thought of her . . .

'Ready?'

She turned quickly to find James standing in the doorway that connected her room to his. He had changed into riding clothes too—the look emphasised that raw maleness that made her heart patter. 'Yes, I'm ready,' she confirmed unsteadily.

'Come on then.' He dropped a casual arm around her shoulder as they walked downstairs and out to the stables.

The horses were already saddled, and eager to be out on the hills. They trotted gently down to the bottom gate, and out into the road leading up out of the valley. The perfect weather was continuing —not a cloud marred the flawless blue of the sky. The hedgerows were alive with crane's-bill and toadflax, and high overhead a kestrel hung effortlessly on the upcurrents of warm air.

Half-way up the road a lane branched off, and she urged Topaz into a steady canter. Behind her she could hear the hoof-falls of the big chestnut, following close. The ground was rising, and a faint breeze stirred her hair. Below her the Levels spread as far as the eye could see, a green and gold patchwork of fields and hedges, rising in the far distance to the blur of the Quantock Hills, while nearer at hand the oval hummock of Glastonbury Tor stood like a perpetual mystery against the sky-line.

She clattered across a cattle-grid covering an ancient narrow ditch, and let the horse find her own way to the top of the hill, past the grubby white sheep that cropped the rough grass. She had always loved to ride up here—it was so wide and open, she felt as though she could reach up her hand and touch the sky.

'What are you doing?' asked James, ripples of laughter in his voice.

She smiled into his eyes. 'Touching the sky. This is the highest point in the whole world,' she told him.

'Oh? Where did you learn geography?' he teased.

She laughed happily. Nothing seemed to matter any more—she didn't care if what she was doing was right or wrong, didn't care what anyone thought of her. She didn't care who James had loved before, nor who he would love next. He was here with her now, and now was all that mattered.

'I'll race you to the copse,' she challenged, spurring Topaz into a gallop. The young horse had a smooth, easy motion, and loved to stretch her legs. She leaned up over her powerful shoulders and let her fly. It was thrilling. The two horses raced neck and neck over the grassy slopes of the hills, the wind whipping their manes, their tails streaming. Cassy could feel the filly's exhilaration, her will to beat the big chestnut; but she didn't quite have the stamina, and inevitably James began to draw ahead.

He reached the trees, and reined in, grinning as Cassy caught up with him. 'I won,' he declared. 'What's my prize?'

She laughed breathlessly. 'What do you want?' she asked.

'What do you think I want?' His voice had suddenly taken on a husky tone, and Cassy felt her cheeks flame scarlet. 'I've been away for two whole days,' he reminded her. He swung down from the saddle. 'Come on.'

Cassy looked down at him, shocked. 'What . . . not here?' she gasped.

'Why not?' he enquired, glancing up at her in mocking challenge.

'But . . . what about the horses?' she temporised.

'They won't be going anywhere, not with all this good grass to graze.'

She stared down at him helplessly. His eyes told her that he would brook no further argument or delay. Her mouth was dry as she slid down into his arms. He held her close, curving her tightly against him so that her breasts were crushed against the hard wall of his chest and she could scarcely breathe. His eyes were burning as they gazed down into hers. 'I want you,' he growled.

His kiss was hungry, invading every corner of her mouth, and she felt an answering hunger rise inside her, as fierce as a forest-fire. She reached up her arms, wrapping them tightly around his neck, clinging to him as if she were falling. Her blood was pounding, her body was like a reed in the wind as his desire swept over her.

With a low moan he broke away from her, and she gazed up at him blankly, wondering what she had done wrong. 'I'd better see to the horses first,' he explained, and she realised that his breathing was a ragged as her own.

She stood watching, breathless with anticipation, as he ran up the horses' stirrups and loosened their saddle-girths, and tucked up their reins so that they wouldn't tread on them. They seemed quite content to crop the grass along with the sheep, and there was little danger of their wandering off up here.

He took her hand in his, and led her down among the trees. There was a hush in the air, as if all the world were waiting for what was going to happen. A hundred yards or so into the wood there was a small clearing around a fallen tree-trunk. The grass was lush and long, never disturbed, and the sweet fragrance of wild violets perfumed the air.

'There. What could be more romantic?' he taunted softly.

It was indeed a lovely spot—the perfect setting. Everything was perfect—except for that mocking note in his voice, reminding her that the dream was flawed. She sat down on the tree-trunk, and unfastened the strap of her riding-helmet, and dragged off her boots.

'Take the grips out of your hair,' he told her. She put her hands, and loosed the pale-gold waves, letting them tumble around her shoulders. 'Beautiful,' he approved, letting one silken strand slide through his fingers. 'Don't wear it up—I like it better this way.'

Slowly he began to unfasten the buttons of her shirt. She held her breath, her eyes focused somewhere around the mid-point of his chest. She could hear the roughened drag of his breathing as he drew the fabric aside, and gazed at the firm, creamy swell of her breasts, hiding in the lace cups of her bra. 'Beautiful.'

Her heart was too full, she couldn't hold back the words any longer. 'I love you, James,' she whispered tremulously.

She had expected him to mock her, and he did. 'You little hypocrite,' he taunted, a bitter edge to his voice. 'You have to convince yourself of that, to ease your old-fashioned conscience, don't you?'

'Oh, James . . .' Blindly she reached out and drew him against her, burying her face against his chest. 'Please . . . I mean it . . .'

He laced his fingers in her hair, and dragged her head back roughly. 'Spare me the Sarah Bernhardt act. I'm not impressed,' he grated harshly. 'Your heart's for sale to whoever pays the right price.'

His mouth closed over hers, crushing her lips apart, and her tears spilled over, coursing down her face. With rough impatience he dragged her shirt back from her shoulders and dropped it somewhere on the ground, and his kisses burned down into the hollow of her throat. Her body was responding, but her mind was torn with despair, and she couldn't stop crying.

He gripped her shoulders, and shook her fiercely. 'Stop it, damn you,' he rasped.

She caught her breath on a sob. 'I'm sorry, I can't help it.' She blinked back her tears, and forced herself to meet those feral dark eyes. 'I *do* love you. I know you don't love me, and I don't expect you to, after . . . after the way I've behaved. You've every reason to think I'm just a mercenary little bitch . . .'

'I do,' he muttered tautly. 'But it doesn't help.' He dragged her back into his arms, and began to kiss the tears from her eyes. 'There's only one way to get you out of my system.'

Her head swam dizzily as he laid her back on the warm grass. Swiftly he stripped off the rest of her clothes, and his eyes blazed as he gazed down at her naked body. She felt herself burning in the flame, and reached out for him, drawing him down to her. Her mouth sought his, urgently, and she moved beneath him in wanton invitation. She pulled off his jumper and threw it away, and her hands ran down over the hard muscles in his back, glorying in his masculine strength.

But part of her still wanted to fight him, angry at the memory of his cruel words, and they rolled over and over in the grass, tussling like a pair of wild animals. He laughed, enjoying the struggle, but when he chose to end it he subdued her resistance easily, pinning her beneath him and taking her with a swiftness that inflamed her desire to white heat.

She cried out as the storm broke over her, stunning her with its force. She seemed to be soaring, sailing high into the sky, stretching out to reach the ultimate heights of pleasure; and then falling, falling, into eddying swirls of darkness, her bones melting and her body aching with a deep throb of satisfaction.

Afterwards she lay beside him, staring bleakly up at the high blue sky. His hurtful words had cut her to the quick. But then she couldn't blame him for being so suspicious of her—she had known that by asking him for the money she was destroying any hope that his desire for her could be translated into something deeper. Now she was going to have to live with that, and make the most of whatever time she had. It would never be long enough.

It was a long time before either of them moved. But eventually Cassy opened her eyes, and eased away from him to sit up. 'Hadn't we better get dressed now?' she asked tentatively. 'The horses . . .'

He rolled over on to his back, heaving a deep sigh of contentment, and looked up at her. 'Do you know, you look the image of that little Sèvres figure, sitting there like that,' he murmured. He lifted one hand, and trailed his finger-tip down the length of her spine. 'Are you a fake too, or are you for real?'

She couldn't answer. She couldn't forget the way she had insisted that she wasn't going to be added to his 'collection'. So much for good intentions!

'Ah well, I suppose you're right. We'd better get moving,' he grunted. 'If we leave them much longer, they'll be going back to their stables alone, and we'll have to walk back.' He got to his feet, picking her up and kissing her lightly before turning her towards her clothes with an intimate little pat on her bare behind. 'Go on, then. You've got grass stains all down your back,' he told her teasingly.

'Oh.' She twisted to look over her shoulder. 'They'll come off in the bath, won't they?'

'I expect so. Do I get to scrub them with soap?'

She slanted him a flirtatious look from beneath her lashes. 'If you want to,' she purred.

He swept her up in his arms, swinging her round. 'The things I want to do to you would fill a book,' he declared. 'But they'd never be able to print it—the words would burn the pages.'

They had three more days together before another business-trip took him to Japan. The first day he was gone she moped around the house, utterly miserable. She didn't even want to go down to visit Grandpa. But the next morning, she forced herself to pull herself together, and after breakfast she sat down to look through the local paper to see if there were any sales in the area worth visiting.

It was another lovely spring day, and she was sitting in the small drawing-room, with the french windows wide open. The dogs were at her feet—she was too glad of their company to send them back to their baskets. Somewhere upstairs she could hear the steady hum of Mrs Bolliver's vacuum cleaner—it always seemed vaguely incongruous to her, but after all a stately home needed to have its carpets swept, its windows cleaned, just as much as any humbler dwelling.

Suddenly Donner gave a low growl, and got to his feet. Cassy looked up in surprise as a familiar stately figure appeared on the terrace. 'Grandpa! You shouldn't have walked all this way!' she gasped, jumping up to help him to an armchair. 'Quiet, Donner. Sit.'

Grandpa set aside his walking-stick, and leaned back, closing his eyes. 'I'll be all right in a minute, when I get my breath back,' he assured her weakly.

'What on earth possessed you to climb that hill?' she protested. 'I was coming down to see you in half an hour.'

'I just wanted to get out of that house for a little while,' he grumbled crotchedly. 'All that noise and dust! I've had it all week—I couldn't stand it a minute longer. I shouldn't have to put up with that at my age.'

She laughed drily. 'You wouldn't if you don't mind getting electrocuted one of these days when you go to switch on a light. Would you like a drop of brandy?'

'I thought you'd never ask,' he returned, a twinkle of mischief in his pale eyes. 'Well, so this is what my fine Sir James has done with my house,' he went on, gazing around the room. 'At least it hasn't been turned into a health-farm, or a school for delinquents—I should be grateful for that much, I suppose.'

She smiled as she poured him a generous shot of brandy. She had hoped to persuade him to come up and see the house sooner or later, and she had been worried about how he would react. But he seemed to be quite philosophical about it.

'I see he's still got my old clock.' He rose to his feet again, and reached for his stick. 'Still going, too. Do you know, that clock was purchased by the second viscount, way back in 1705.' He moved on around the room. 'My, he's got some expensive stuff in here. It'd keep me awake at night, worrying about burglars.'

'That's what I thought. But he's got a good security system.'

'Huh. That'd be even worse, living in a bank-vault.'

Cassy laughed. 'It isn't that bad, honestly. Look, you'd hardly notice it.' She showed him the thin wire that ran around the window-frame. 'If it had been switched on when you came in, the police would have been here in five minutes,' she told him.

'What if you forget to turn it on?' he challenged.

'It's on an automatic timer—it's only a problem if you want to go for a walk in the evening, and forget to trip the manual override. And the dogs have been known to set it off accidentally from time to time.'

'I bet the police don't like that very much,' he observed lugubriously.

'Oh, if there's a mistake, we always ring straight away and let them know,' she explained. She stroked Donner's sleek head. 'You're a nuisance, aren't you?' she said to him. The dog wagged his tail, happily accepting the compliment.

'Nice dogs,' Grandpa commented, sitting down and coaxing the dogs to come to him. 'I expect they're good guard dogs.'

Cassy laughed. 'Actually they're as soft as butter,' she admitted wryly. 'If a real burglar came, they'd probably lick him to death.' Grandpa had clearly won their canine hearts by finding exactly the right place under their ears to tickle. 'This is Donner,' she told him, 'and that one's Blitzen.'

He chuckled richly. 'Donner and Blitzen, eh? Yes, I like that. So he's got a sense of humour, young Clayton?'

Cassy couldn't supress a small smile of reminiscence. 'Yes, he has,' she agreed.

'And are you going to marry him?' he asked sharply.

A scarlet blush spread up over her cheeks. 'Oh . . . well, I don't know . . .'

'You know what I think about this set-up,' he chided censoriously. 'I let you do as you wished, but I'm beginning to think it's time I had a few words with this Sir James of yours, enquired into his intentions.'

'Oh, Grandpa, I'd really rather you didn't,' she protested quickly.

He shook his head. 'I'm afraid I've no time for these lax modern ways,' he reminded her. 'It would never have been heard of in my day.'

Cassy sighed. James was going to be furious if Grandpa, of all people, started upbraiding him about his morals. And the last thing she wanted was a quarrel between the two men. But with luck, Grandpa would forget all about it again. 'Are you going to stay for lunch?' she asked.

'I thought you were coming down to have lunch with me?'

'Well, yes, if you like. Are you ready to walk

back yet?'

'Of course I am. I don't think I'm boasting when
I say that I'm remarkably fit for my age. And anyway, it's easier walking down the hill.'

James returned from Japan with a little jade
trinket-box for her. She accepted it with mixed
feelings—did he think that so long as he brought
her a present from every trip she would be content
to sit idly at home? 'It's lovely—thank you,' she
murmured.

He put a hand under her chin and tilted her face
up to look at him. 'What's up?' he asked in a voice
that would brook no evasions.

'It's just . . .' She took a deep breath. 'Look, I
can't just sit around here, like a doll waiting to be
taken out of a box.'

A flicker of sardonic amusement crossed his
face. 'Getting bored? Well, I suppose that's under-
standable—it must be pretty dull for you, stuck
down here in the back end of Somerset after the
bright lights of Manhattan. Never mind—I have to
go up to London next week, so you can come with
me.'

She hesitated for an instant—she really ought to
pursue the subject now that she had raised it. But
James had other activities on his mind, and for
some time it was really quite impossible to think
rationally about anything.

And somehow as the days passed she kept
finding excuses not to discuss the problem. It was
easier just to live in the present—forget the way
this affair had begun, forget the problems the
future was inevitably going to bring. She didn't
even try to tell him that she loved him.

*   *   *

It was fun to go up to London. She had only ever been there to stay once before—on a school trip, years ago. James had a small service flat in Kensington—very luxurious, with a deep-pile white carpet and lots of bronzed glass.

'What a fabulous place,' she observed, gazing round in awe.

'Do you think so? I think it's a bit over the top, myself, but I don't spend a lot of time here. I've a meeting this afternoon—what are you going to do with yourself?'

'Oh, I don't know. I might do a bit of shopping,' she mused.

'OK. We'll have dinner somewhere nice this evening, maybe go to the theatre—what do you fancy? There's bound to be at least three Lloyd-Webbers running in town.'

'That would be nice,' she agreed, smiling up at him. 'I'll see you later then. Have a good meeting.'

'Right.' He caught her to him, and kissed her firmly on the mouth. 'I'll be back about six.'

When he was gone, she unpacked the clothes she had brought—Rhoda had sent most of her stuff over from New York by now, so she had a much better selection to choose from than in the beginning. Then she picked up her handbag and hurried out.

There were several sales advertised in the Trade Gazette that might be worth a visit. Even if she didn't buy anything today, it would give her a chance to look around, get the feel of the auction-rooms, start to make herself known to the auctioneers and—possibly more important—the porters.

She had a very interesting afternoon, though she

didn't buy anything, but she kept an eye on her watch, and got back to the flat by five o'clock—plenty of time to have a bath and get changed before James came home. She chose to wear a black satin trouser-suit, cut on masculine lines, with a white silk blouse and a shoe-lace tie, and she left her hair in loose curls around her shoulders, the way James liked it.

But six o'clock came and went, with no sign of him. She put the television on and sat down to watch the news. Half past six . . . seven o'clock . . . Where on earth had he got to? She didn't even know where his meeting was, so she couldn't ring and check that he was all right.

By half past seven she was prowling impatiently round the flat, fuelling her anger with resentment. It was always the same—he expected her to wait around on his damned convenience! If he had a shred of decency he'd have taken a moment to ring her and let her know he was going to be late.

At half past eight he did finally ring. 'Cassy? I'm sorry—I'll be a bit late.'

'A bit?' She forced herself to swallow her irritation. 'You said you'd be home by six.'

'Did I?' At least he sounded apologetic. 'Oh, yes—we were going out to dinner, weren't we? Never mind—get yourself something to eat out of the fridge. I'll snatch something on the way home.'

'All right.'

He must have caught the plaintive note in her voice. 'I'm really sorry, Cassy,' he said gently. 'Look, we'll go out tomorrow night, OK? I'll book the table and the theatre seats first thing in the morning.'

He was trying to bribe her again—make everything all right by spending money on her. But all she wanted was his time. 'I don't mind about not going out,' she protested, the words tumbling out unplanned. 'I just wanted to spend the evening with you. That's why I came up to London with you—not for the bright lights and the shopping.'

He laughed softly. 'A candlelit dinner for two, alone in the flat?' he teased. 'How romantic!'

'I told you before, James, I love you,' she blurted out, her voice shaking with the tears that were choking her throat. 'I know that you don't believe me, not after I asked you for all that money. But I *had* to have it. Grandpa owed it to Michael Farrell, you see, and he was threatening to take him to court over it. It would have killed Grandpa. And then there was the house—it was your own fault, you were going to throw him out on the street.'

'Whoa there!' he protested. 'I wouldn't have thrown him out. I didn't even know that my legal department were dealing with the determination of the lease—it was just administrative routine. I've got hundreds of properties—I can't oversee every one personally, it would be an impossible task. But before any action could have been taken they'd have had to come to me for the go-ahed, and I wouldn't have given it. What do you take me for?'

She hesitated. 'You . . . you wouldn't?' she whispered.

'I suppose that old goat has been filling your head with stories about my wickedness,' he went on drily. 'At one time he was putting about some cock-and-bull story that my grandfather had cheated him out of his money. Fortunately no one believed him.'

'I did,' she confessed in a small voice.

He laughed aloud. 'You? You've got more sense than that!'

'I didn't have when I was ten years old,' she pointed out. 'I grew up on Grandpa's stories—what would you expect me to do but believe them? It wasn't until just a few weeks ago that he finally told me the truth.'

'Oh, Cassy! Why didn't you guess?'

'I . . . I don't know. I suppose I must have been quite naïve—but Grandpa's the only family I've ever had. He brought me up. I knew he gambled a bit, but I never realised how bad it was, not till I came home this time. He deliberately kept it from me. If I'd known, I'd never have gone to New York, for a start.'

He was silent for a moment, and then said, 'It looks as though we've got quite a lot to talk about, Cassy. But not over the phone. I have to go now, but I'll be home as soon as I can.'

Something in the tone of his voice made her heart skip. 'Yes,' she agreed readily. 'Goodbye, then.'

'Goodbye.'

She put the phone down, and sat staring at it, an odd little quiver fluttering in the pit of her stomach. Anger, and not being able to see his face, had made her say the things she had been bottling up for weeks. And this time he seemed to believe her! She hardly dared to let herself hope . . .

She was too excited to eat anything. She paced around the flat like a caged tiger, looking at her watch every five minutes, checking her appearance in the mirror a dozen times and wondering if she ought to change into something different—

something a little more feminine, perhaps.

At last she heard the sound of his key in the front door. She ran out into the hall to meet him, her heart soaring. 'James . . .!'

'Good evening, Cassy.' The grim expression on his face knocked her back in shock. She stared at him blankly.

'What . . . what's wrong?' she stammered.

'You'd better pack your things. We're going back to Somerset,' he told her bluntly.

'Tonight? But . . . but why?'

'There's been a burglary.'

Icy fingers were curling around her heart. 'A burglary? At Bradley Park?' she asked weakly.

'That's right. Hurry up and get ready. I'm leaving in five minutes.'

Numbly she obeyed him, too bewildered by what had happened to be able to think straight. They didn't speak as they rode down in the lift and walked through the echoing undergound car park to where he had left the Aston Martin, nor throughout the long drive home.

CHAPTER TEN

THEY could see the flashing blue light of a panda-car through the trees as they came up the drive. There were two more outside the front door, and the house was crawling with police. James drew the car to a halt, and came round to open her door for her.

Coleman, the butler, was hovering in the hall, and he came forward as soon as he saw them, relief mingling with consternation on his face. 'Oh, Sir James, thank goodness you're home!'

'Did they get much?' asked James crisply.

He shook his head. 'They knew what they were after. They've only taken the best pieces—the Imari jars, the long-case clock from the small drawing-room.'

James frowned. 'The clock? That's a pretty big item to sneak away with. How did they do it?'

'They had a van. The police have found tyre-marks at the side of the house. I'm most terribly sorry, sir. I was watching television early this evening.'

'OK, Coleman. Where's the Inspector?'

'He's in the small drawing-room,' the butler told him, leading the way. 'That's where they got in.'

There were two plain-clothes detectives in the room. The elder, a stocky, grey-haired man in a creased suit, came forward and offered James his hand. 'Good evening, sir. I'm glad you could get home so quickly.'

'How did they get in?' James asked him as they walked into the small drawing-room.

'The french window has been forced.'

'What about the burglar alarm? Or the dogs, come to that?'

The detective smiled wryly. 'That's one of the reasons we suspect it was an inside job. Not only must they have known what sort of security you have, but the dogs didn't bark. It must have been someone they knew.'

Behind them, Cassy paused on the threshold, staring at the armchair. She had had a sudden vivid image of Grandpa sitting there, stroking the dogs, talking about the burglar alarm . . . *No!* It wasn't possible—Grandpa would never do a thing like that!

Fortunately James and the detective were deep in a examination of the broken window-catch, and hadn't noticed her momentary abstraction. She had regained her composure by the time they turned round again.

'Who knew that you were going to be away?' the detective was asking.

James laughed drily. 'All my staff here at the house, and anyone they may have spoken to; similarly anyone at my office; Cassy's family, I expect. Maybe two or three hundred people in all.'

'I see. Well, that doesn't help us very much,' the detective agreed. 'Well when the boys from forensic get here we'll see if they can turn up anything. Not that I'm very optimistic—this was done by a very professional firm.'

Cassy felt a secret relief at his words. Of course—it was ridiculous even to think of Grandpa being involved.

'Your servants, Sir James,' the detective was going on. 'How long have they been with you?'

'Let me see . . .' With a wave of his hand he invited the detective to take a seat. 'Coleman was the most recent arrival—he's been here three years now. Greening—my chauffeur—he's worked for me for eight years. The domestic staff have all been here for many years—they worked for my grandfather.'

The detective nodded. 'Mmm.' He slanted an enquiring glance towards Cassy. 'And the young lady . . .?'

Cassy blinked at him in astonishment. Surely he didn't suspect . . .? But then of course, it was his job to suspect everyone. 'Miss Durward has been staying with me for a few weeks,' responded James, telling the whole story in those few words.

'Miss Durward?' His voice suddenly held a note of extra respect. 'Of course—you must be the Viscount Bradley's granddaughter. I'm sorry—I hadn't realised.'

She smiled at him, insensibly relieved. Just for that fleeting moment, it had been a horrible feeling to be under suspicion.

'This clock, Sir James. How much would it have been worth?'

Cassy didn't pay much more attention to the discussion between the two men. Her mind had gone back to this afternoon's telephone conversation with James. If only they could have talked like that before—so many misunderstandings could have been cleared up. It was a shame that this unpleasant incident had spoilt the evening—naturally all James's thoughts were wrapped up in that at the moment. But later—then they could talk.

It was almost dawn when the police finally left, leaving instructions that nothing in the small drawing-room was to be touched until the forensic people had been. Coleman and Mrs Bolliver had made their statements and long-since retired to their own quarters, and as the last of the police-cars disappeared down the drive a silence settled over the house.

'Well,' she began diffidently. 'I think I'll go up and get ready for bed.' James didn't answer. 'Are you coming up?' she asked.

He turned to look at her, and the expression in his dark eyes chilled her to the marrow. 'Come into the study,' he said tersely. 'I want to talk to you.'

She followed him into his business-room off the hall, her mind in turmoil. When he had said 'we have a lot to talk about' before, over the telephone, he had had a warm note in his voice, but all trace of that was gone now. She was at a loss to know what was wrong.

'Sit down,' he instructed in a toneless voice. She perched on the edge of a chair as he sat down behind the big antique desk. 'Right,' he began without preamble. 'The police have gone now, so you can tell me the truth.'

She stared at him blankly.

'What do you know about this?' he asked.

'No more than you do,' she answered, aghast. 'Surely you don't think *I* had anything to do with it?'

'Did you?'

'No, I did not!' she retorted hotly. 'How dare you?'

'All the evidence points to the conclusion that they had detailed inside information—and that they were familiar enough to the dogs to prevent them from barking. Who would you suggest? Coleman? Greening? Mrs Bolliver, perhaps?'

Again that uncomfortable thought of Grandpa crossed her mind. What if it was him? James was watching her steadily, waiting for an answer. She thrust the guilty thought to the back of her mind, and rounded on him in anger. 'How could it possibly have been me?' she demanded. 'You know perfectly well that I was in London with you.'

'So you were. What a convenient alibi.'

She rose to her feet. 'I don't have to listen to this!'

'Where are you going?'

'To pack my things,' she stormed furiously. 'I'm not staying in this house another minute!'

'Oh yes, you are.' The tone of his voice stopped her dead in her tracks. 'You stay until I tell you you can go.'

'I *beg* your pardon?' she queried tautly. 'You can't keep me prisoner here!'

His cruel mouth curled into a chilling sneer. 'You have alternative accommodation? For yourself *and* your grandfather?'

She sat down again with a bump. 'You . . . You wouldn't!' she breathed.

'That was part of our original contract,' he pointed out coldly. 'I agreed that he could stay on sufferance for the duration of our affair.'

'Yes, but . . . you said last night that you wouldn't have evicted him.'

'The rules have changed now.'

She was shaking. What had gone wrong? Last night, after they had spoken on the phone, it had begun to seem that everything was at last starting to go right. And now it was worse than ever. 'If . . . if you think I was involved in the burglary, how on earth can you even consider having me around?' she asked, a tremor of unshed tears in her voice.

'Because I'm oddly reluctant to let you get away with killing two birds with one stone,' he told her, an inflection of chilling mockery in his voice.

For a long moment they stared at each other across the wide desk, like two fencers waiting for the *coup de grâce*. Cassy was the first to drop her gaze. 'I hate you,' she whispered tightly.

'Go to bed.'

She obeyed his terse dismissal, trailing slowly up to her room like an automaton. Her heart felt as heavy as lead. If he came upstairs, expecting to come into her room . . .

But he didn't come, not that night nor any of the subsequent nights. By day he treated her with a distant politeness that she found difficult to handle, never referring to the burglary, or their contract. He only went away twice, and then only for one night. The rest of the time she felt as if she were virtually under house-arrest.

Since it seemed that she would have few opportunities to get to any more sales for a while, she made arrangements to ship over the stuff she had already bought. Rhoda was delighted with it.

'Well done, honey,' she enthused over the phone. 'Everything went almost before I'd unpacked it. Marsha took the table—she just fell in love with it on sight.'

'What about the bottle-vase?' Cassy asked, a smile in her voice.

'Oh, yes, well . . . I thought I'd hang on to that, just for a little while. When can I expect the next batch?'

'Oh, not for a while I'm afraid. Oh, sorry, Rhoda, I have to go now.' She had just heard James's car in the drive—he had been up to Bath. 'I'll ring you next week.'

'OK. 'Bye, honey. And give that hunky man of yours a great big kiss for me—or better still, bring him over here and I'll do it myself.' She chuckled richly.

'Well, maybe, one day,' Cassy murmured evasively. 'Goodbye, Rhoda.' She put the phone down quickly as James came in through the front door, looking up at him with a smile that she knew was over-bright.

There was no answering smile. 'I want to talk to you,' he said brusquely.

Her heart thudded. *Now* what? It was more than two weeks since the burglary, and she had felt as if she had been living at the north pole. He went into his office, and reluctantly she walked across the

hall and stood in the doorway. 'What do you
want?' she asked, hoping she sounded cool and
composed.

'Shut the door.'

She did as she was bid, and then turned to face
him defiantly. He took a piece of paper from his
inside pocket, and held it out to her. She took it
from him, and glanced at it curiously. It was a
photocopy of the bill of lading she had signed when
sending her consignment of antiques to Rhoda.

'Well?'

'Well what?' she enquired acidly. 'Do I have to
ask your permission for everything I do?'

'That depends on what you're doing,' he responded. 'What was in the consignment?'

'It's listed on here,' she pointed out, handing the
paper back to him. 'Antiques.'

'I can see that. Antiques that very conveniently
don't need an export licence.' He took another
paper from his pocket and handed it to her. It was
another photocopy—this time a bill of sale . . .
from an auction-room in Palm Beach, Florida . . .
for a long-case clock, made by Tompion and
Banger in 1705 . . . with a provenance stating that it
had been the property of the Right Honourable the
Viscount Bradley.

'A remarkable coincidence, don't you think, my
dear?' he enquired drily.

'W . . . where did you get these?' she asked.

'I felt the police might be a little too busy to pay
a great deal of attention to one stolen antique
clock—a fact which you were no doubt relying on.

So I employed a private detective agency.'

She sank weakly into the chair beside the desk.
'You think it was me, don't you?' She looked up at
him with a bleak expression. 'You really think that
I would steal your stupid clock?'

'How else would you explain these documents?'

'If your spook had been a little more assiduous
in his investigations, he could have found that out,'
she observed bitterly. 'At least about this one.' She
pointed to the bill of lading. 'I don't know
anything about the other one, but this one's quite
straightforward. I bought the things at an antique
fair in Wells a few weeks ago—while you were in
Spain. I've got the receipts upstairs. I sent them to
Rhoda—and she's sold them, so she'll have
receipts too.'

He frowned. 'What were you buying antiques
for Rhoda for? You don't work for her any more.'

'I know,' she retorted, her eyes glittering with
anger. 'All you wanted me to do was sit around
here like some harem-slave, waiting on your every
whim. Well, I'm sorry, but I'm just not cut out for
that sort of life—I don't want to turn into a cab-
bage. I wanted something to do, so I arranged with
Rhoda that I would buy for her on a commission
basis.'

He frowned. 'So what was the big secret about
that? Why didn't you just tell me what you wanted
to do?'

'Because *you* said I couldn't get a job!' she threw
back at him in exasperation.

'Not a job, no. I didn't want you going off to
Bath or something five days a week. You know the

way I have to operate, going off abroad at short notice, sometimes for days at a time. If you had a job too, there'd have been times when we might have hardly seen each other for weeks on end. That's no way to keep a relationship going, as I've found out time and again, to my cost! But going to sales and auctions while I was away—I wouldn't have minded that.'

'Well, how was I expected to know that?' she demanded furiously. 'You were behaving like the Tsar of Russia, handing out your orders.'

He looked genuinely surprised. 'Me?'

'Yes, you! Just because you could hold out the threat of evicting Grandpa, like a sword over my head.'

'And because I paid you forty thousand pounds,' he reminded her, effectively silencing her. He picked up the other paper. 'And you still haven't explained this,' he pointed out.

She shook her head. 'I told you, I don't know anything about that.'

His dark eyes captured hers and held them with that black-magic spell. 'Nothing?'

She shifted uncomfortably in her seat, unable to evade that searching gaze. She felt as if he could see everything that was in her mind—even that tiny niggling doubt about Grandpa.

'Have you ever invited anyone up here while I've been away?' he asked.

She could feel the colour draining slowly from her cheeks. 'No. Well . . . only . . . Grandpa came up once.' A flicker of interest in his eyes told her that he was rushing to conclusions. 'But Grandpa would never . . .'

'Which rooms did he go into?'

'Only . . . only the small drawing-room,' she admitted in a small voice.

'He saw the clock?'

She nodded reluctantly. 'He . . . he said it must be like living in a bank-vault.'

'So you showed him the security system?'

'Yes.'

'And he met the dogs?'

'He wouldn't . . . No, I don't believe it!'

'Oh yes, he would. If the bookies were braying, he'd do anything.' He took her wrist in a firm grip, and hauled her to her feet. 'I think it's about time we had a few words with your grandfather,' he added grimly.

'No! James, stop,' she begged breathlessly. She had to run to keep up with him as he dragged her across the hall and out of the front door. 'James, don't be angry with him, please. He's just an old man.'

'I'm not angry,' he asserted tersely.

'James, please . . .' But he strode on, through the trees, pushing open the wicket-gate and dragging her with him down the rough path to Grandpa's back garden. 'If you upset him . . .' she hissed warningly.

'Upset *him?*' He shoved open the back door so violently that it slammed back noisily against the wall. Cassy had a fleeting glimpse of two shocked faces in the kitchen as James hauled her up the stairs.

Grandpa glanced up, startled, as the door of his

sitting-room burst open unceremoniously. The guilty look that passed across his eyes dispelled Cassy's last hope that she had been wrong. But he was still blustering. 'Well! To what do I owe this honour?' he demanded, drawing himself up with towering dignity.

She ran over and knelt down beside his chair, taking his hand, 'Grandpa, you know why we're here, don't you?' she asked gently.

'N . . . no, of course not. How could I?' he protested indignantly. 'But now that you *are* here, young man, I'll take leave to enquire of you what your intentions are towards my granddaughter.'

'Grandpa, this is serious,' Cassy interrupted him. 'You remember when you came up to the house, I told you about the burglar alarm? Have you talked to anyone else about it?'

He looked from her to James and back again, and slowly the bluster drained out of him. His shoulders sagged in defeat. 'I'm sorry, Cassy, really I am. But there wasn't anything I could do. It was Michael,' he explained, real tears sparkling at the corners of his eyes. 'I owed him money, you see.'

'But Grandpa, I paid him back,' she reminded him.

'I know, I know. But . . . well, it was too good a chance to pass up. I'd got really good odds, you see—fifteen to one. They were shortening right down—seven to four, second favourite. But then it was scratched, right at the last minute.'

She frowned in confusion.

'I imagine he was hoping to recoup his fortunes

on the Derby,' James supplied drily.

Grandpa nodded. 'I would have, too—that horse couldn't lose. I could have paid Michael back the stake-money, and have had enough left over to buy the lease on the house.' He shook his head sadly. 'But it didn't work out—and he was threatening to take me to court for the money. There was no way I would have paid him, so he said . . . he said he'd let me off, if I did what he wanted.'

Tears rose to Cassy's eyes. 'Oh, Grandpa,' she sighed, hugging him.

He patted her shoulder. 'You know, I think he only did it to spite you, for not marrying him—he didn't need the money.'

'I wouldn't put it past him,' she agreed bitterly. 'I wouldn't put anything past him.'

'Where's Farrell now?' asked James.

'He's gone—gone abroad. The police were after him for a whole load of other things.' He put up his hand and brushed a tear from the corner of his eye. 'Your old Grandpa's just a silly old fool,' he admitted penitently. 'But I've really learned my lesson this time, I can tell you.'

'Oh Grandpa, you said that before,' she reminded him with a wistful smile.

'I know, I know. But this time I really mean it—I swear it, on my dearest Elizabeth's grave.'

She hugged him lovingly. 'Grandpa, you really are an old goat!' she murmured, shaking her head.

'Well, that's a nice thing to say!' he protested indignantly.

She gurgled with laughter, relieved to see him regaining his spirits. 'Well, it's true,' she insisted.

'You've lied to me, you've lost thousands and thousands of pounds gambling, and now you've got yourself tangled up in a burglary! You'll be lucky if James . . .' Suddenly she noticed that James had gone. She scrambled to her feet, and ran to the window, just in time to see the garden gate closing.

'I could do with a . . .' Grandpa began.

Cassy picked up the brandy-decanter and pushed it into his hands as she ran from the room. She raced down the stairs and across the garden, and out on to the path. 'James!' she called frantically, racing to catch up with him. 'Wait, please.'

He turned at the sound of her voice.

'Oh, James, I'm sorry,' she gasped breathlessly. 'I would never have believed that Grandpa could do such a terrible thing. But please. Don't say that everything's over between us.'

'Over? No—not unless you want it to be.'

'*I* want it to be?'

'Yes. I wouldn't blame you—after the things I've accused you of.'

She stared up at him. 'You had every reason to,' she whispered. 'It must have seemed . . . What are you going to do about Grandpa?'

He smiled down at her. 'Don't worry,' he assured her, 'I'm not going to tell the police. They won't catch Farrell now, and as for your grandfather—well, he's just a pathetic old man. I feel sorry for him. He can't help himself—he's a gambling addict, he has been all his life. He was ripe for a man like Farrell to pluck.'

'I . . . I didn't expect you to be so understanding,'

she confessed tremulously.

'Which just goes to show how much you've mis-judged me.'

'Yes . . . yes I did.' Her heart was racing out of control.

'And I misjudged you, Cassy,' he said gently. 'I thought you were a gambler too—especially after I saw you with Farrell. He's quite notorious, you know. When I saw the way you were behaving with him, I was afraid he had some kind of hold over you—I should have guessed it was through your grandfather. Did he really want to marry you?'

'Yes, he did,' she confirmed with a shudder.

He drew her into his arms. 'And I thought you were scheming to marry money. I was determined not to let you make a fool of me. But I couldn't help myself, even when I thought you'd proved me right by asking for that forty grand. All I knew was that if you were in trouble, I wanted to protect you.'

Her eyes were sparkling as she gazed up into his. 'It was no wonder you thought I was a mercenary bitch,' she whispered. 'But I . . . I think I would have ended up being your mistress anyway.' A faint blush suffused her cheeks, and she focused all her attention on the knot of his silk tie, putting up her hands to give it an unnecessary adjustment. 'I . . . I can go on being your mistress, can't I?' she pleaded.

'No.'

Her eyes flew back to his.

'It isn't enough,' he grated fiercely. 'It was never enough. You've got to be my wife.'

Somerset had moved unexpectedly into the earthquake zone. She stared up at him, stunned. 'Your . . . your wife?' she repeated weakly.

'Yes. Damned fool that I am to trust a Durward, but I love you.'

'You do?'

For answer he gathered her up, and his mouth claimed hers in a kiss that was pure tenderness. She clung to him, dazed by the sudden reversal.

'But . . . you said you *weren't* going to marry me,' she protested when he let her go.

He laughed with a trace of self-mockery. 'I did, didn't I? And I meant it at the time.' His fingers curled in her hair, tipping her head back ruthlessly. 'But if you take after your grandfather . . . he threatened.

'I don't . . . Oh, I don't!' she promised, her eyes alight with happiness.

He smiled down at her. 'No, I don't think you do. Well, now we've finally got ourselves sorted out . . .' He swept her into a dizzying embrace, plundering the deepest corners of her mouth in a kiss that sent her heart into orbit. She responded with feeling, excitement thrilling through her like a nuclear reaction.

With a low growl he pushed her back against a tree, his hand roving freely down over the curves of her body. He was making his intentions abundantly plain, and she fought for a shred of sanity, trying to push him away. 'James,' she whispered, shocked. 'Not here.'

'Why not?'

'It . . . it's broad daylight.' He had unbuttoned

her shirt, and found the front clasp of her bra, and
unfastened that too. She closed her eyes as he
brushed the fabric aside to fondle her naked
breasts. 'James, don't . . . what if someone
comes?' But she was melting beneath his expert
touch as his fingers nipped gently at the sweetly
sensitive buds of her nipples.

'No one ever comes this way. And anyway, I
don't give a damn. I want you—right now.'

He had dragged her skirt half-way up to her
waist when she heard footsteps on the path below
them. 'James! James, stop it! There *is* someone
coming,' she whispered desperately.

As she flustered to do up her buttons, she saw
over his shoulder the startled face of Miss Tucker,
who worked in the newsagents, one of the biggest
gossips in the village.

'Good evening, Sir James,' the good woman
said, looking from one to the other, her lips a thin
line of disapproval.

James leaned his hand against the tree, sheltering
Cassy a little from her sight. 'Good evening, Miss
Tucker,' he responded politely, unable to look at
her as he fought to contain the laughter that was
rising inside him.

'Good evening, Cassy.'

'Oh, er . . . hello, Miss Tucker. Where are you
off to?' Cassy managed with a polite smile.

'I'm taking the short cut over to Long Acre
Farm. That new paper-boy forgot to deliver Mr
Newsome's *Angling Times*.'

'Really?' murmured James. 'Well, don't let us
keep you.' Cassy flashed him a warning glance, her

lips tightly clamped together to stop herself giggling.

'No. Well, I'll be seeing you both in church on Sunday, no doubt.' She stalked away, censure in every line of her back.

As soon as she had vanished round a bend in the trees, Cassy collapsed, helplessly laughing. 'Oh, my goodness! You should have seen her face!'

'I couldn't let myself look,' he confessed. 'How much did she see?'

'Enough. It'll be all over the village by nightfall. I'll never be able to hold my head up again!'

He smiled down at her. 'Do you really care?' he teased her.

'Not a bit!' she confessed gaily. 'I love you, and I'm not a bit ashamed of what I've done.'

He hugged her fiercely. 'That's the spirit,' he approved warmly. 'Anyway, by tomorrow all they'll be talking about is the great big wedding we're going to have.'

She gazed up at him happily. 'It doesn't have to be a big one,' she said. 'We could slip away to the register office.'

'Are you joking? We'd never be forgiven. No, you have to wear a long white frock, and I have to wear a morning suit, and we have to have at least five hundred guests.'

'I can't wear white,' she protested. 'I've been living with you for weeks!'

He scooped her up in his arms, and carried her up the path as if she weighed nothing at all. 'And at least half a dozen bridesmaids,' he went on, ignoring her objections. 'And a coach and four white horses to take you to the church. And a wedding cake with three tiers. And dozens of crates of champagne. And lots of long, boring speeches . . .'

Harlequin American Romance

Romances that go one step farther . . . American Romance

Realistic stories involving people you can relate to and care about.

Compelling relationships between the mature men and women of today's world.

Romances that capture the core of genuine emotions between a man and a woman.

Join us each month for four new titles wherever paperback books are sold.
Enter the world of American Romance.

𝓗arlequin 𝓢uperromance

**Here are the longer, more involving stories you
have been waiting for... Superromance.**

Modern, believable novels of love, full of the complex
joys and heartaches of real people.

Intriguing conflicts based on today's constantly
changing life-styles.

Four new titles every month.
Available wherever paperbacks are sold.

 Harlequin Books

You're never too young to enjoy romance. Harlequin for you . . . and Keepsake, young-adult romances destined to win hearts, for your daughter.

Pick one up today and start your daughter on her journey into the wonderful world of romance.

Two new titles to choose from each month.

Harlequin Presents

Coming Next Month

Available in March wherever paperback books are sold, or through
Harlequin Reader Service:

In the U.S.
901 Fuhrmann Blvd.
P.O. Box 1397
Buffalo, N.Y. 14240-1397

In Canada
P.O. Box 603
Fort Erie, Ontario
L2A 5X3